Benjamin Wachs

A Guide to Bars and Nightlife in the Sacred City

STRANGE CASTLE PRESS
San Francisco

Published by Strange Castle Press
San Francisco 2014
All rights reserved.

Edited by Janet Shepard
Proofread by Mark Faber
Design by Norma Tennis

FIRST EDITION

978-0-9793270-7-0

Cover images courtesy of istockphoto

Printed in the United States of America

10 9 8 7 6 5 4 3 2 1

Contents

Preface

Each city is a neighborhood in the collective unconscious.
— Jorge Luis Borges

I FIRST DISCOVERED THE SACRED CITY JUST BEFORE
the turn of the millennium, when I was a freelance
nightlife reporter for Playboy.com. I was traveling across
America, and then Europe, and then Russia, and then the
Middle East, waking up each morning not knowing which
city I would fall asleep in. I would dream of Venice before
drinking at Belgian bars, and have visions of Jerusalem in
Prague. Cities became pieces of a jigsaw puzzle, connect-
ing in ways that you could not see on a map to reveal the
secret order of the universe.

If God is in all of us then there is more divinity in a
city of 10 million souls than there is in Stonehenge, the
pyramids, or a sliver of the True Cross. Cities pulse with
rough love unevenly spaced over boulevards and across
alleys. If we tape enough heartfelt wishes on streetlights
and leave enough dreams on the curb, anything can
happen. Millions of souls in crowded neighborhoods
praying beneath the surface of their daily lives lead
to manifestations of the miraculous and infernal just
around the corner. A block of Paris where fire dancers

spin outside Notre Dame connects to a sliver of Chicago where angels dance in a speakeasy, that attaches to miraculous Thai food in London, and to a faith healing in San Francisco, to an architectural marvel in Moscow, and a tantric revelation in New Orleans, to a lost opera in Vienna and a resurrection in Pittsburgh and the perfect couch appearing on Craigslist in Toronto. Never stopping.

This is the Sacred City.

A Guide to
Bars and Nightlife
in the
Sacred City

The High Prices in Venice

VENICE IS EASY TO GET LOST IN. LIKE ANY MEDIEVAL city, it was designed for people who are going to spend their whole lives there, and then eternity after they're finally raised from the dead. That was the Godly plan, but commerce came and the city became home to heathens and heretics and philosophers, art and courtesans and carnival.

The City has a sinister hold on me. The thousand carnival masks staring at me out of shops, across courtyards, with empty eyes, were trying to tell me that this was the Devil's summer home, and if I waited too long the Master would return.

I believed them, but I didn't leave.

Instead I bedded a raven-haired prostitute in a small room off the Rialto, and for some reason she stuck around, finding me each morning, following me on my walks around the city, negotiating good prices for me with the Italian merchants, and holding my hand while she said inscrutable things in halting English. At night the sex was overwhelming. Our bodies attacked each other. And then she slipped away, I don't know where, only to find me

1

again in the morning and step out from the shadow of a church to kiss my cheek.

Once I asked her to stay the whole night and she laughed. "Why? For love?" I never asked again.

I got lost every day, crossing the canals and slipping behind alleys, dashing into a hundred churches all of which seemed empty, and hearing the voices of carnival masks whisper alchemical secrets in my ear as I stepped back into the sun. "The city is sinking," they warned me, "but if you stay long enough, we will teach you how to turn lead into gold."

I hadn't paid her for weeks, and still she found me each morning. She wanted little: I bought her lunch and dinner, I paid for wine and dessert, and sometimes I gave her a token of my affection if we danced. I asked her why she came back.

"Why?" she asked. "It was my birthday when I met you."

She showed me the master glassblowers. I watched just inside the door of their workshops as they heated ovens hot as hell, then sculpted liquid glass. They could make a rose or a human face so easily, but they preferred abstract shapes. They apprenticed themselves by imitating the world as it is. Then they proved themselves by designing pieces of a new world. I saw the shape of love curved in pink glass with blue rings orbiting its ending; I saw temptation wrapped into a sharp curl and made the sting of a violet wasp; I saw emotions I had never imagined suspended in green, surrounded by pockets of air.

I told the glassblower I wanted to know what these things felt like. He told me that if I have grandchildren, perhaps they will understand.

2

One glassblower showed me a wave of perfectly clear glass bending through time to collapse in a sulfurous crag of dark red and fiery black.

"It is your future," he told me, "just as the masks describe it." He offered it to me for $1,000 U.S. I haggled him down to $780, and had it wrapped carefully in silk. I walked back outside and she found me. She took my arm and followed where I led. I saw that the masks were closing in, hanging closer to me on every wall I passed.

The sex was especially good that night.

I had planned to spend six months seeing the mountains of Switzerland, the valleys of France and the forests of Germany. Instead I had been in Venice four and a half months now. The summer was coming. The Devil drew near.

New wines arrived by truckload from across Italy, where they were loaded on boats and sent up the canals to be put in the cellars of underground bars that served uncommon varietals. She took me on a tour. I found my favorites. We drank together, looking for the flavors that made us forget the island was sinking. Another month. I learned how to get from my hotel to the glassblower's workshop, to the Piazza San Marco, to the best of the shady wine bars, without missing a turn. Even at night, without a moon, I almost never got lost. I noticed gargoyles hanging from the walls of houses for the first time. The gargoyles whispered, too. I slept through the church bells in the morning. The hotel maid began to wake me up in the afternoon. I cursed at her in Italian. She crossed herself and didn't come back.

The maid was the hotel owner's wife. The next morning, long after my raven-haired demon had slipped out, the state police opened my door. I had stayed in Italy for five months on a one-month visa. The police grabbed my suitcases as they were, leaving most of my clothes behind, and escorted me down to the street. I would be sent on a flight back to America immediately. I cursed at them, I pleaded. I begged them. I almost wailed "But the Devil is coming soon!" But they were state police, not Venetian, and they served another master.

As they shoved me into the back of the car, inspiration struck.

"You must let me shop!" I screamed. I offered them $2,000 U.S. for a few hours buying souvenirs from my favorite places. The plane didn't leave for another six hours, and the money was good, so they escorted me wherever I asked. It was the only time I ever traveled on wheels in the city of canals.

I went to the glassblowers' shops. I purchased the shape of love, I purchased the sting of temptation, and I bought the emotions I had never imagined, suspended in their prison of green. I put them all in my suitcase. I could not take my future with me, because it had been left back at the hotel, and already stolen by the maid when an officer went back to look for it.

I went to the wine bars and bought the rarest bottles. I went to the mask makers and stood in their shops and listened...listened...to find the masks that whispered to me the loudest. I bought 13 of them before my credit card declined to serve me. I arranged to have them shipped back to the States. If I was being taken out of Venice, I would bring as much of Venice with me as I could. From inside the last shop, I saw my raven-haired woman sitting at a café, sipping brandy, watching me through the window. I ran to her, followed by the police. She pretended not to know me.

"One kiss," I begged.

"Why?" she asked. "For love?"

The policemen laughed at me. Stupid American. The masks...the masks...were quiet.

Not even the stewardesses spoke to me on the flight home: They knew what I was. An American consular official asked if my rights had been violated in jail. My rights? What did I care? I wanted to stay and that was all.

The flight stopped in London, and by the time it touched down again in Washington I'd realized that I was broke and homeless and couldn't remember the English pronunciation of my name. I heard it again for the first time when I was finally released and sent on my way, with nowhere to go.

I'd spent it all, stopped paying my rent months ago... even the treasures I put myself in debt to take back would be delivered to my sister's house in Minneapolis. A land of snow.

I lived in a homeless shelter for a while. I got a job in Human Resources and pulled myself out of debt. I rented a house far out in the suburbs.

I have the boxes from Italy stored in a locked room behind exercise equipment. I haven't opened them. I'm not allowed to go back to Italy for another three years. I tell myself it's better that way. I believe it. I say my very English name over and over again.

When I'm in a city at night, if I'm not careful, if I'm too deep in thought or not paying attention to one foot after the other, I look up to find that I've walked an old pattern...from my hotel to the glassblower's workshop, to the Piazza San Marco, to the best of the shady wine bars, without missing a turn.

Every time I pass a church I look to see if she's waiting in the shadow, and I have never fallen in love.

The Funeral of Abbott Casparus

IT IS TRADITIONAL FOR MONKS OF THE CISTERCIAN order to create some item for the public good. For centuries the Abbey of Stift Heiligenkreuz has manufactured bricks for the local people to use; the Carthusian Abbey produces cheese; the monks of Scourmont Abbey make beer.

In the morning, and at night, they chant hymns and Bible verses in complicated, ecstatic harmonies.

Monks are only human, and I was in attendance at the Brabant Abbey for the funeral of Abbot Casparus. I pretended to be a spiritual tourist, jaded and cynical, when in fact I was a pilgrim. I pretended to be decadent, when in fact I was eyeing celibacy with the same ardor I had once reserved for powerful-seeming women in bars. Please, I asked silently, show me a depth and strength that I can believe in, rather than one more wall made of crumbling resolve.

I was there, the monks sympathetic but bothered by me, when they buried their old and worldly abbot, and brought out casks of brandy they had made by hand as an act of devotion to God. I was there, uninvited, in the corner, and not a drop touched my lips as they passed around the goblets and told stories in French of the wisdom of the dead. I saw the tears, and I heard the laughter, as man after man took enough solace to make his legs wobbly and his eyes weak.

I was the first man to hear the bell calling for night services—I do not know who sounded it. I watched them look around, and try to stumble to their feet. I watched them, mumbling in French, until Brother Karsten made a decision, and pointed to the crucifix mounted in the banquet hall. I saw them all gradually turn to face it.

I saw them, as one, begin their drunken plain chant; I heard their voices, in perfect symmetry, recall the words of their faith, and then I wept, because it was even more beautiful than it had been the night before, their intoxicated harmonies filled with simple love. And I wept because I knew I could never be one of them.

I left the next morning—they gave me bread and cheese—and went back to Brussels, where I found a bar, drank the brandy made by monks, and told lies once again. This story, that music, is the only thing you really know about me.

A Moment in Moscow

HAVE YOU FORGOTTEN ME? WE SPENT THE NIGHT together once after meeting in a Moscow bar and romping across the city. You asked me a question about alchemy, of all things, alchemy, and then told me the story of the lover who'd tried to kill himself after you left. We walked down the empty street beneath a bitterly cold moon at 3 a.m. and were passed by a pack of dogs going to war. We kissed and you asked if I could stay another night, but I couldn't, and then...somehow...I told you exactly what you needed to hear, my head becoming a philosopher's stone and curing you of all the trauma that had brought you to my arms.

It was a process I've never forgotten, or been able to repeat, and I wonder, sometimes, what would have happened if I'd said I would stay a second night.

But when I saw you, in Paris, taking pictures for a fashion magazine—living the dream you'd told me about over cocktails—you only saw me as someone blocking your shot. And I wonder if I've changed so much, or if you've just forgotten what I look like.

The Napkins
of Zurich

IT'S A LITTLE KNOWN ACCIDENT OF HISTORY THAT the renowned theologian Albrecht Berringer and the Nobel Prize-winning mathematician Marcus Sloan met in the bar of a Swiss hotel in 1951. They were attending separate conferences: Sloan a small forum of thinkers on fractals (what would later be known as the Zurich Discussions), Berringer a symposium on peace in our time that utterly failed to predict the full bad faith of the Soviet Union.

Berringer had a legendary sexual appetite while Sloan had been celibate after the death of his young wife, and those who knew them suggest that their meeting would have been quite unlikely, as even in the same bar they would have been looking for different experiences. Hildebrand suggested that they were introduced by the bartender, who was an admirer of both their work. We do know that Berringer was drinking a single malt scotch on the rocks, while Sloan nursed a gin and tonic.

However they were introduced, what followed was a 19-hour discussion about whether it was possible to quantify the impact of the divine on human affairs: to establish a model whereby even if one could not see the presence of the divine directly, it would be possible on purely probabilistic grounds to say "God must have been involved there." Those 19 hours account for Sloan's famous absence from the Zurich Discussions during Volkoff's infamous digression on the nature of intelligence.

I am in possession of the only extant artifact of this 19-hour interlude: the three cocktail napkins on which they wrote their theses, maxims, and equations. I encountered them at the Delphic Bookshop in Zurich on Hoogstradt, which has somehow managed to endure even as the historic buildings surrounding it have been repurposed into strip clubs and fast-food emporiums. They were kept under glass and hung above the "philosophy and poetry" section. I inquired as to what they were, and when I was told, I insisted that I had to purchase them. It took a great deal of haggling, but I believe the owner, a Herr Shattuck, was harder up than his pride would let him admit, and it only took two hours of discussion before I walked out with the napkins under glass and an early edition of Goethe.

Sloan's math is beyond me, and Berringer had a habit of writing in Latin, which I cannot read, so the set is purely a historical artifact for me, rather than an intellectual insight trapped in amber. But Hildebrand tells me the conclusion they finally came to, after bringing the full weight of their intellectual traditions to bear on the problem.

According to Hildebrand, Sloan and Berringer reluctantly concluded in hour 16 that while it was not possible to prove God, it was possible to effectively disprove mathematics—the fact that mathematics can often correctly make predictions being of no more conclusive proof than the fact that alcoholics are frequently cured after they find God. They spent the next three hours going over their proofs to make sure that nothing had been missed, then angrily tossed their napkin notes to the bartender. They left to return to their respective conferences and never spoke again.

I have no idea if this is true, of course. I have only an artifact and the word of a knowledgeable source. The rest I reluctantly take on faith.

Dance of the Seers

I HAD A GLASS OF GRAND MARNIER WAITING FOR Occam the Magnificent when he walked in at 8 p.m. sharp. He'd told me last week when he'd arrive: "8 p.m. sharp," he'd said, "after my 7:30 appointment cancels because of a sick child." He sat down next to Madam Wehrstehl.

"I'm saving that seat for a friend," the lean old woman said, nursing her gin and tonic, not looking up at him. She only drank the good stuff, top shelf, and she took a long time.

He sat down. "No, you're not," he growled through his bulldog face. "No one else will sit here tonight."

"Look underneath you," she muttered.

He stood up and saw, for the first time, a Tarot card placed upon the seat. Death. He turned pale. "I'm sorry," he said, "I didn't see that coming." He slid a stool over. They didn't look at each other.

Miss Babylon walked up to the bar in a low-cut black dress with a bare back—she has to have sexual chemistry with someone before reading them—and asked for another vodka cran.

They say that if you have one jewelry shop on the street it's a store; if you have two jewelry shops on the same street it's a competition; and if you have three jewelry stores on the same street it's the jewelry district. Districts are good for business and not even psychics can overcome the laws of economics. The good ones drink together— not because they like each other, but because no one else is worth drinking with. No one else really understands them—especially not the poseurs.

I put her glass underneath the tap. "Drinking a little heavy tonight?" I asked. She nodded. "I hope it's nothing…" I began, but she interrupted me.

"Don't," she said. "Just don't."

"Okay," I said.

She shook her head, and I saw now that her eyes were red and puffy. "Soon," she said. "Too soon."

I put the glass on the counter. "Okay," I said. "This one's on the house."

She sighed and walked back to her table with Mr. Malcolm the palmist and Dorian Wonderful, who they call "the boy wonder" behind his back because he used to really be something and then he turned 30 and became kind of a big deal on cable access and lost his gift somewhere between tapings. If one of these other guys lost the gift, they'd leave and never come back here: they'd be free and ashamed at once. But Dorian keeps coming back, keeps trying to fake it with the one group of people on earth he can never hope to fool. I don't think I helped Miss Babylon out at all. Somehow, I think I made it worse.

"Do you know," Occam the Magnificent told me, his hands flat on the bar, "that Grand Marnier is the drink of truth?"

I walked over and started polishing some glasses to keep busy. "I did not know that."

He lifted his glass up, swirled the orange-amber liquid around, then put it to his lips, carefully keeping his pencil mustache dry. "Indeed," he said when his sip was finished. "And do you know why that's important?"

I picked up another glass. "I do not."

"Because there's a difference," he said, "between knowing the future and telling the truth about it."

"I can see that," I said, although I'm not sure I could. It didn't matter: he's one of the ones who gets lost easily in his own world. "Can I get you anything?" I asked Madam Wehrstehl, although I knew it'd be another half-hour before she ordered her second drink. Nothing psychic about that. She waved me away.

Snagging this gig was one of the best moments of my life. They say it was destined, but they say things like that. I came to Seattle not really believing I had a future. I came to the city, like so many young people do, thinking I had the ins-and-outs of life figured and there weren't any surprises left. I was a bad painter, and a pretty good graduate student in philosophy when I showed up for class, and a solid dancer for an amateur. But I've always gotten by on my looks and the fact that I make a drink that doesn't taste half as stiff as it is. I don't put on airs: I know my strengths. I was coasting, the way young people who never got the knack of working hard do. I could always fall back on being a bartender.

This job pays the best: these people aren't rich, but they're really particular about their bartender. They're really particular about the hands they brush against as they take their liquid comfort. They're willing to pay a premium to get what they want, willing to put up their tips and wages to make sure they can keep it. The owner hired me because, he told me, I'm going to die alone. Alone and abandoned. Apparently that's what they look for.

Dorian Wonderful got up and walked over. His walk's gotten cockier since success on TV, but his bright blue eyes are more cautious and constantly darting since he lost his touch. I filled a little glass bowl full of trail mix and passed it over to him. "What'll it be?"

"Long Island."

"Sure thing." I did a little slide over to the proper bottles. It must be because I'd just been thinking about dancing. I kept the liquor light. He likes to be seen drinking more than he likes to drink.

"I've got a YouTube channel now," he said.

"Yeah? Fantastic."

"Doing readings of local celebrities," he said. "Councilwoman Godden, Dennis from Channel 5. I got one with Henry Rollins when he was in town, which was really cool. I'm going to be on an NPR segment next week out of the local studio."

"Wow," I said, shaking the mixer. "Things have really picked up for you."

"Yeah," he said, looking around nervously. "Yeah." He wasn't standing anywhere near Occam or Madam Wehrstehl. He leaned forward over the bar. I poured his drink, put it on the counter and slid it over to him, leaning in close. "You know what I've discovered?" he whispered.

"What?"

"It's easier to do promotion when you don't really have anything to promote."

"Huh."

I looked over at the table he'd come from, where Mr. Malcolm's bald head was leaning in close to Miss Babylon: it looked like they were having an intense conversation. "They want anything?"

He thought about it. "Yeah," he said. "Give me another round to take back."

I got the glasses, made the pours, and handed him the drinks. He took them back to the table without paying. Nobody has to pay cash-in-hand. Only regulars drink here, and they all get tabs. Knowing when your tab is due without being told is what makes you a regular.

At the other side of the bar, Occam let out a big sigh. I stepped back over and got out the bottle of Grand Marnier. They like it when you don't have to ask. I started to pour.

"You know what that weasel won't tell you?" Occam asked. I shook my head. "It's not just promotion," he said, though there's no way he could have heard those whispers. "The more important thing is: it's easier to love when you don't know. It really is."

"Ah," said Madam Wehrstehl. She held the Lovers card in between her bony fingers. "Ah yes." She flipped the card around once...twice...three times.

"It's always better not to know," Occam said.

"Ah, yes," she replied, turning the card around one more time, returning it to its original position.

"Pity Miss Babylon," Occam said.

Madam Wehrstehl put the card away.

* * *

They stayed late that night, and everybody drank more

19

than usual, until one by one they stumbled out. First Mr. Malcolm, then Dorian Wonderful. Then Occam the Magnificent and Madam Wehrstehl gave each other a look and she picked the Death card up off the stool and they walked out. Not together but at the same time.

Only Miss Babylon was left, half in her cups. Since they're all regulars you need to treat them gently, and I waited a while. But she just sat there with half a beer, staring at the wall.

"I'll call you a cab," I said at last, picking up the phone.

She looked up. "Don't," she said. I put the phone down. She stood up. "It's over," she said. "It's all over." She took a deep breath. "This is going to hurt."

I waited. She walked towards the bar. "Do you know what you're like? To us?"

I shook my head.

"You just reek of loneliness and abandonment that you haven't even felt yet. You radiate it. It comes off you like heat. It just…" she stepped closer and shook her head.

I shrugged. A little bit. "I like all of you." It seemed like the only thing to say to that.

"We like you too, for a pretty boy," she said. "But it… your fate…" She stepped closer. "Someone would have to be really…really…self-destructive to get close to you."

She leaned over the bar. "You're very pretty." She kissed me for a long time.

It was the best sex of my life. They tell me it won't be worth it.

Free Will

THE BELL JAR USED TO BE A NEWSPAPER BAR, THE place that stayed open late because the rush came at midnight when the morning edition was being put to bed and all the reporters needed to find something to do before they went home. Now it's where you go when you want to speak to the dead.

I'm here because my kitchen is too clean. That's how I know something's wrong. When the carving board smells like oak and you can eat off the floor and the 30-piece set of German cutlery is sharpened to a lethal edge, it means there's something cooking in my mind that I don't want to taste yet. My kitchen's been too clean for a long time. I've only just now run out of stains to wipe away.

I recognize a few people here, from a long time ago. The thin man in a black sweater, his head balding, always drinks French beer and drums his fingers on the bar. The redheaded woman with a scar across her cheek is looking for a fight: I remember her once standing over a man she'd beaten to the ground with a broken bottle of merlot, daring us to do something about it. She blew me a bloody kiss that night. The man in the white suit is new. He looks like the devil in a movie about New Orleans. The girl in the dark red velvet cocktail dress reading a book, she's either a prostitute or has a story to tell.

The man in white walks over to me, which feels like a violation of some code, and gets on my very large bad side. "I notice," he says, and his voice has an affectation as though he's trying too hard not to have an accent, "that you're drinking a brandy of particular note."

My kitchen has a little balcony that lets me watch the sun set over the Potomac. That moment where the green trees turn rose red like a glass of wine in my hand is the most beautiful thing I have in my life. For a while, I thought it was enough. I really did. That's what I think of, instead of answering him.

"I don't know my brandy," he goes on. "Not like I'm guessing you do. But I saw the conversation you had about it with my friend," he gestures to the bartender. "I saw him get it from the back room. I saw him blow the dust off it, and I see that the label is in a language I can't read."

"A white suit's nothing but overkill," I say to the air. "It's hard to look at a man in a suit like that without laughing."

The redhead with the scar looks up, wondering if trouble's brewing. But he picks up as if nothing happened. "I don't know much about much in this world," he says, "but I do know I like to talk to people who have much better taste in liquor than I do."

I wet my lips on the glass…just enough to let it burn, just enough to let the scent of it poison the air…and then put it down. "Schopenhauer," I say, not looking at him. "If you know something about the philosophy of Arthur Schopenhauer, then I'll tell you about the drink. Otherwise you get nothing."

He blinks and grins. "How odd. But I can do you one better."

"You've got nothing," I say, and turn back to the brandy.

"Amanda!" he calls.

The girl in the velvet cocktail dress looks up.

"Show him what you're reading," he says.

She holds up the book. *The World as Will and Representation,* by Arthur Schopenhauer.

"This," he says, preening, "is a bit of a coincidence."

I stare at the book as though it were the queen in a game of three-card-monte. I wonder if she has a whole library down her cleavage and pulls the right volume out for the right occasion. Dangerous thoughts. Maybe I shouldn't have left home.

"I believe," he says, sitting a bar stool over, "that you owe me a conversation."

I scowl. I look away.

Amanda stands, waiting to see what happens: or maybe she already knows, the way she had just the right book.

I take a breath. Let's do this. "This brandy comes from a small distillery in Haiti that was opened by the first French colonialists and run by monks up until the take-over by Papa Doc in 1957. He loved the brandy but he couldn't have Christians running the place, so he rededicated the compound to Baron La Croix, the spirit of sex and death, and kept it open. Every few months he'd have a ceremony there, something wicked to remind the church who was in charge. Later, when his kid Baby Doc was overthrown in the '80s, the rebels burned it down. But there was a cellar deep underground that contained 100 bottles of the good stuff, from back in Papa Doc's day. I brought one of those bottles in here 15 years ago and left it with the owner, just in case I ever needed it."

Her jaw's dropped. He's smiling so wide he could bite me. The redhead with the scar is still listening, waiting for her cue to break something. Only the balding man in black is ignoring us all.

"That can't be true," Amanda says.

"That can't be Schopenhauer," I say.

"I believe every word," the man in white says.

She sits down next to him.

"The implication," the man in white says, "is that now you need it."

I nod, slowly. "Maybe."

He reaches over and picks up his mixed drink. It looks like a gin-and-something. He holds it up in the air. "To Baron La Croix," he says, "the founder of our feast."

Amanda considers, then holds up her glass of red wine. I take a lot longer, but eventually I hold up the snifter, and we all drink. God, it burns...it burns so good, every addictive thing about immolation condensed into a liquid, rolling down my throat. Oh, God. I have to take it slowly. I have to. The rest of the bottle is still waiting for me, if I ask.

"How did you get it?" he asks me when I put the glass down.

I look away. "I said I'd tell you about the drink. That's all."

He leans forward. "You meant it then," he says. "But you don't mean it now."

"The hell I don't."

"A conversation is like a fine meal," he says. "It's easier to say no if you don't taste it. Once you've had your first bite, it's so much harder to put your fork down." He smiles just that way again. "You've tasted, and if you were going to abstain I doubt you'd be here."

Godammit, he's right. This man is not the strutting poser I took him for. But I don't want to give him the satisfaction.

Amanda leans forward. "Why did you want to talk about Schopenhauer?" she asks.

She's got that creamy complexion I could just dip my hands into—she's got the kind of womanly curves I used to get into fights over. The kind of girl I used to break things for. And she's asking the right question. I've been telling myself for years now that beauty liberates the spirit and is the answer to addictions…and here she is, asking just the right question while I drink, and suddenly I can't see the sunset from my balcony in my mind anymore.

I lean forward. I let my look linger down her dress. Either she'll like it or it'll push her away. I can live with both. "Why do you have that book?" I ask. "That's the trade-off." The man in white is right: I don't want to drink alone anymore.

She grins shyly and looks away for a moment—the move is so alluring, it practically screams "jump me." And I should be more upset that these thoughts are all coming back so easily. The question is if she's doing it on purpose.

"I'm a graduate student," she says. "An MBA."

I nod. The man in white nods. Across the room, the bartender nods.

"Okay," she says, "It's…okay, I have this one asshole professor. Well, they're all assholes, but he's the worst. He's one of those business guys who thinks that anything that isn't making money is for sub-humans—you know, only losers have feelings. And half the time, whenever somebody says something in class about ethics or how the world should work, he'll say 'This isn't Schopenhauer.' 'This is business, this isn't Schopenhauer.' I got so…fucking… sick of it that I actually decided to read Schopenhauer, just so that…" She laughs. "Okay, I don't know. Maybe someday I'll have a comeback. Or maybe it's just one of those things you do to feel like you're in control again. You know? Fuck you: I'm reading Schopenhauer. This IS Schopenhauer!" She cradled her head in her hands. "So that's it."

"Ahhhhhh," says the man in white. "I think that's beautiful."

She flashes him a smile. A strange smile. A smile I can't read.

"Your turn," she says.

I turn away. "It's personal."

She laughs, a little. "Well, yeah. I mean, God, after your answer to his question? The 100-year-old voodoo brandy from Haiti? I figure this is going to be awesome."

"Oh, it is," the man in white says. "I'm sure it is."

I'm trying to ignore him. "You didn't believe me," I tell her.

"It doesn't matter," she says. "But…do you really not want to tell it?"

"He does," says the man in white. "His dignity just needs

an excuse. And he owes us now, so everybody gets what they want."

I take a deep breath. I pick up my snifter, pour liquid immolation down my throat. Really...if I'm honest...this is what I came here to say. Somehow he knows it.

"Some people can't stop what they start. Some guys have a choice of not drinking, or closing every bar on the block. Some guys have the choice between celibacy or debauchery—but nothing in between. They can't hold hands in the movie theater and make out on her front porch. That's not a choice they can put weight on: it's like trying to grab on to air when you're falling down an elevator shaft. Some people are either saint or sinner, and it has less to do with morality than how hot it is one afternoon and what they smell on the street corner in the morning. Coffee? Saint. Bacon? Sinner. He could just as easily spend all his money on children's antibiotics as he could shipping off to Afghanistan with the mercenaries who make orphans. It just depends on how hot the wind is and what it carries. Or he can decide not to leave his apartment that day. Do you get that? The real choice isn't *orphanage* or *mercenary,* it's whether to stay indoors and clean your kitchen instead of walking outside." I point at Amanda. "Got it?"

She blinks, but she keeps staring at me. I suddenly wonder if she has any tattoos.

"I understand perfectly," says the man in white.

"You're just saying that to act like you're keeping up," I say.

"You're just here to make trouble," he says. He smiles.

Amanda gets up off her stool and stands between us. She throws *The World as Will and Representation* down on the bar. "I'm listening," she says.

She's close to me now. I can smell her skin. It smells like she has one tattoo on her back: probably a butterfly.

I pick up where I left off. "If you're one of those guys, you're probably going to die young. But maybe you don't. Maybe you get very, very good at living in the margins. In the extremes. Maybe you're so good that you live long enough to get perspective: you decide you want to be a saint rather than a sinner. What do you do?"

"What do you do?" the man in white repeats.

I drain the remainder of my brandy and then throw the snifter down on the floor behind the bar, hard. The bartender looks over, sharply. I point at the man in white. "He did it," I say. "Bring me another." Yes, another. Liquid lava, another glass, burning away everything in its path. The bartender considers, and first gets a dustpan and broom to sweep up behind the bar. Good for him. Amanda giggles. The man in white is still smiling, damn it. Everybody else is looking at us except for the balding guy. He drums his fingers on the bar...we'll never crack his reserve. The redhead is grinning like her favorite song's been put on the juke box.

"Everybody's got a suggestion," I say, "for how you can live your life. But there are really only two people who can help you. Sigmund Freud and Arthur Schopenhauer. They're your best friends."

They give me blank stares. Fuckers. I shouldn't even talk to them.

The bartender finishes sweeping up the glass shards and dumps them in the trash. He gives me a stare, then goes into the back room where my bottle is kept. When did I make the decision to tap this drink? When I walked in the bar? When I left my kitchen? When I noticed that there was nothing in it left to clean? When did my footsteps stop being something I made and become something I followed?

I realize I'm still talking. I'm like a music box, too tightly wound. "They're the guys who figured free will out. It's not something you're born with, it's not something you get automatically: it's something you develop, it's something you have to practice. And until you do, you're at the mercy of every impulse you have. You think you're making decisions, but you're being played by your mind and your body and your blood. To get free will you have to be smart, and work hard, and practice watching every single instinct until you can see them coming in advance and actually make real choices before the impulse reaches you, and it's too late. They both agree on that: they both tell you how. But here's the difference..."

I want to stop, but the words keep rushing out.

"Freud never said free will would make us happy, just more responsible. And I fucking want to be happy."

Amanda nods. "Me too."

"And that's why I need Schopenhauer. He understood that pure aesthetic pleasures...art, good food, nature... can bring us joy even after we've learned how to manage all our other instincts. You can become a saint and still get to experience heaven on earth. And I was so...so...

29

tired of leaving a body count. I wanted a piece of that. So I tried it."

The bartender brings the bottle back over, along with a new glass, and pours. I don't tell him to stop, but he does anyway after the pour gets big. I like this kid. I toss him a five. I hope I don't end up breaking his face tonight. "I tried it," I say again. "I mastered it all. For seven years I lived without any pleasures except the aesthetic ones. I didn't drink except wine with dinner, but I learned how to be a great cook. I didn't go out to movies, but I had an apartment with an amazing view. I didn't..." I stare at Amanda. I stare all over Amanda. "I didn't have sex, but I listened to Mozart and Ravel and Brahms. I read great books. And...I'm telling you...I was free."

I pick up the snifter and swirl the brandy around, holding it in front of my eyes. "I was the most free man you'd ever met, because I was in charge of every impulse in my brain. I decided which shelf everything went on, and how long it stayed here. I lived like a rich hermit, but I was my own master. And...I wish it had lasted."

I take another drink.

"But the truth is that for maybe two years now I've been treading water. Being free isn't enough. It's not... satisfying, after a while. And I don't...I don't know what to do about it. I've been trying not to admit it to myself." God, I've turned the bar into a therapist's office. Somebody needs to kick my ass. "So I do some more reading and I see, in a journal, that Schopenhauer frequented brothels. He..." I shake my head. I laugh at myself, under my breath. "That son of a bitch. He was getting some on the side. Where's that in the book, huh, Arthur?"

I slam my hand down on Amanda's copy of *The World as Will and Representation*. "So that's why I want to talk about Schopenhauer. Now what do you have to say?"

She stares at me for a moment, at my hand on her book, and then laughs. "You're fucking awesome," she says. "You're, like, the coolest person I've ever met in a bar. Hands down."

I scowl. "You don't understand a word I'm saying, do you?"

"Oh dear," says the man in white.

"Why do you think I'm here?" she asks me. "Come on, I've been trying to save my soul through literature and you're the first person I've met who I can actually discuss one of my books with, and you think I'm not paying attention?"

I stare at her, hard. And this time I'm not looking at the skin edging her dress. "So…" I say. "What do you think about the book?"

The man in white leans his head in closer.

She hesitates. "I couldn't do it," she says at last. "I couldn't live that way. Freedom's not worth it."

I pound my hand on the bar. My brandy glass jumps, and I catch it with my other hand. "I knew it!" I say, and put the brandy down gently. "You're not really reading it at all. I'm a drowning man, you're a tourist. You're not looking for a new way to live, you just want to have some exotic stories to tell your buddies at B-school."

She looks offended for a moment. Then she grins and taps her long nails on the book cover. "Maybe I'm just not as self-destructive as you."

31

We lock eyes. And something load-bearing inside me collapses. "I've got a mind to take that book and spank you with it," I growl.

She doesn't blink. "Do you have a hard-cover copy? Because that would work better."

I stand up and reach down the bar to grab her hair. But she leans back and the man in white steps between us.

"You haven't got permission…yet," he says.

I stare back and forth between them. "What?" My hands are clenched in fists.

Amanda pouts. "I need his permission," she says.

He smirks. "That is correct."

Everybody in the bar is staring at us. I ignore him. "What is he, your pimp?"

"That's disgusting!" she says. With relish.

"So, what?"

She shrugs. "I owe him."

"What does that mean?"

She shakes her head.

"That," he says, "is between us. All you really care about is that you need my permission to touch her. And I'll be happy to give it. I want this to work out for you."

"So we're good," I say, knowing it's not true.

He smiles. "Not quite."

I suddenly get it. "You want my brandy. Well…"

He shakes his head. "Not at all."

"I do," Amanda says.

"That's between the two of you." He leans closer to me. "All I ask, for her succulent flesh, the kind you haven't tasted in so long…is for you to call me Baron La Croix, and remember who you belong to."

I jump back. I can't help myself. It's like I've touched fire. "Bullshit!"

"That's all I want." He strokes Amanda's back.

"That's such...such...you're a sick fuck!"

"You don't have to believe me."

"I don't believe you!"

"Good. I'm happy being just an opportunist with obscure kicks."

"This is the biggest bullshit I've ever heard in my life." I'm sweating.

"All I want is to hear you say it."

"Fuck off."

"For her," he says, and strokes Amanda's back again, and she squirms, and I can't remember the last time I wanted something so much, except for a drink.

"Amanda," I say reaching out, but she slips back. Gives me a tsk tsk tsk.

"I want it," she whispers. "Just tell him what he wants to hear."

"But I..." I look back at him. His suit's catching the light just so, it's hard to see his face now. "Why that?"

"Because it pleases me," he says. "Or maybe it's real. Maybe you came here and opened a bottle of brandy dedicated to me by a favorite son. Maybe the sound of the cork popping out, the smell of liquid fire meeting the air, brought me here. Maybe you opened that bottle, and I appeared, and I remembered you, from a time when you used to belong to me, and I want my whole family to be back together again. Or maybe I don't like

Schopenhauer. Maybe that's why. Does it matter? Aren't we having this conversation because you don't care about 'why' anymore?"

I look away. "I don't…I worked so hard to be my own man."

"You decided it was a mistake. That's why you're here." He shrugs. "Call me Baron La Croix, toast to my service, and take the girl. Curse me under your breath, shred pictures of me, come back with a gun when you're finished. Do whatever you were going to do anyway. Just call me Baron, before you do. Acknowledge whose you are."

He reaches out…and strokes my hair. He's fucking…I shudder and pull away. My teeth clench as his fingers lose contact.

He smiles. She laughs.

"It's not like you have a choice," he says. "You made this decision hours ago, maybe days. You said so yourself: you weren't happy being free. Your last real choice put you on this path, and now you're here."

I shake my head again. My throat is dry. I'm drenched with sweat.

"I want you to be happy. But I don't like your pretensions," he says. "Say my name."

I shake my head.

"Say my name." He doesn't need to shout.

"I have a choice," I whisper.

Amanda squirms.

"No," he says happily. "Not anymore."

I shake my head again.

He opens his arms.

Amanda blows me a kiss.

"I have a choice," I whisper. And then I scream.

I scream. I charge. I push past him. Past her. I charge over to the redhead with the scar. I slam into her. I push her off the stool. She stumbles into the wall. I follow, and throw a punch. She ducks, and my hand breaks the wood. She slams a knee into my stomach, and it's on. Oh God it's on. She's incredible. I rip her shirt off before she breaks my nose and knocks me down. I grab her legs and pull. We're bruised and fucking, right in front of them, when the police come. And I never called out anyone's name. I spit blood on his white suit as they pull us into the squad car.

The Red Light of San Francisco

INSIDE, IT SMELLS LIKE PATENT LEATHER, FRESHLY polished, shiny and black. Outside, it smells like fresh rain, just passed, worms on the sidewalk, grass flowering. The two worlds could not touch without something getting ruined.

"Once upon a time," she whispers in my ear, "this brothel was haunted."

"House," I correct. I reach my hand out to the iced tea, grab the shiny glass, and touch it to my lips. Ridges all over, invisible little glass bubbles that my lips can feel. It tastes like peach. I put it down. I don't like things sweetened.

She sighs and runs her hands along her corset. It, too, has ridges all over. "If you could make fine distinctions, you wouldn't be here."

Somewhere outside, clouds part, and the rosy beams of a sunset slip through. For a moment, the room turns red. "It's a house now," I say. "You're the only spirit left."

Her hands caress her long leather boots. "Men," she says, a little disgusted.

"From 1919 to 1938," I say, "this was a warehouse filled with Chinese women stitching purses. In 1939, my great-grandfather patented a machine to create the linings in women's handbags. It revolutionized the industry. He made a fortune, and put all the ladies here out of work. Most left, a few stayed, with nowhere else to go, and when the sailors came through to and from the war in 1940, the women were desperate. What happened next was a kind of natural pattern, like icicles forming on a roof in winter. They sold themselves to save themselves. But here's what's surprising."

I pick the ivory cigarette case off the dresser. The top is engraved with a Chinese dragon, and a cross. I've always wondered about the combination. Was it made for a missionary? Did it come from a vision? An artist playing with symbols he didn't understand? I flip the lid open, take out a cigarette, tap it three times on the case, and put it in my mouth. "Light me," I say.

She tosses me a steel lighter with the Playboy rabbit on it. "You get what you pay for," she says sarcastically. She leans forward, showing me everything underneath the corset, trying just a little too hard.

I catch the lighter in one hand, and flick it open. The flame goes higher than it should. "Pay attention," I tell her. "At the end of this story, you're not here. At the end of this story, you'll never come here again."

"You think this is your house?" she asks. Her hair, dyed deep red, almost matching her lips, tumbles over her shoulders.

I take a deep drag on the cigarette, and blow a smoke ring. It circles lazily up to the ceiling. "The surprising thing," I say, "is how well the story went. Most icicles never last through winter, most brothels never make anyone happy. But this one had a lucky charm, the right combination of sweet sailor boys away from home for the first time and desperate young Chinese women who looked exotic, and they made money. All through the war they made money, and they weren't too unhappy, and the women stayed friends, and then when the war was over and the sailors went away, they sold the business to some white women whose husbands never came home, and they went south. They went south to Los Angeles to open a restaurant, south to Mexico to live near warm waters, south and were happily never heard from again. You get the idea."

She stretches out her arms, with long black leather gloves covering her hands. The smell of leather and woman is driving out the rain. "Most men have trouble opening up. You talk too much." She tilts her head, her red, red hair cascading. "Does that make you feminine?"

I blow smoke in her face. She doesn't blink. "The building changed hands in the 1950s, and in the 1960s, but the business stayed the same. Got more professional. As fetishes caught the imagination, all this..." I toss my hand at her chest and run it over her corset "...came in demand. Very big with stockbrokers in the 80s. The 80s! Do you see what that means? 40 years of continuous operation, men constantly walking in and out, women sweating pieces of themselves into the furniture, and yet almost no tragedy. That's... incredible. It lasted until the fire in '91. The warehouse burned down, unrecoverable. The owner... still a woman, if you can believe that... died, along with three working girls. There was a police investigation, no insurance money, the property lay abandoned for years, until the housing boom early this century, when investors who don't know anything about history saw an opportunity, and converted the lot into six houses. This is one of them. One of six. Houses. This isn't a brothel anymore, it's a home."

Her eyes narrow.

I tap my cigarette into the ashtray and take her all in with a look. "And the fact that you're here, that you're always here, eager and ignorant…well…I'm just trying to figure out who you are."

The scent of leather turns to the scent of char. She throws a glass of iced tea at me, it misses by just a finger. She reaches out and slaps me, knocking the cigarette out of my mouth and on to the floor. Dangerous! Fire! Another natural pattern!

"I guess you like it rough," she says. She reaches over to the armoire for a thick wooden cane. I aim my fist at her throat. The room goes black, then flickers like rapid blinking.

She wakes up from her dream. She's dressed in her satin nightgown, and doesn't own a corset or a pair of leather boots. She's never touched a cane. Her hair is its natural color. Somewhere outside, clouds part and the rosy beams of a sunrise slip through. For a moment, the room turns red. She rubs her eyes, gasps a little underneath the canopy of her four poster bed, and wonders about the man in her dream: where I came from, and if I looked like anyone she knows.

Thanatos Cuisine

THE CHILI CRAB CURRY IS SPICY AND MAKES YOU tear up but you can't stop eating. It walks the line between pleasure and pain, a sadomasochistic dish. It's Chef Pellinore's specialty.

Twelve years ago he went through a bad breakup. She told him the only reason she'd hung in there the last year and a half was that his cooking was so good. It almost made up for the sex, she said.

He carried that around a long time. When the man she'd left him for broke her heart, she came back to him. He refused to make her comfort food. Instead he found himself wondering how unpleasant he could make a dish that she'd still eat. Then he worked to find new ways to make an unpleasant meal too tempting not to eat. He worked like a machinist on meth to develop food that would convince her to hurt herself.

It worked. The mussels were so hot she cried after the first one and screamed after the third, but the flavor came through and she took eleven before she collapsed on the floor and begged for a glass of milk. The corn chowder induced slow nausea but she still ate enough to bend over the toilet for half an hour, and then she crept out of bed in the middle of the night to the fridge and snuck some more, and paid for that, too.

He'd never slept so well.

She figured out what he was doing and it hastened their final breakup but made him more focused than ever on getting his own kitchen. He was a better lover now that he was making dishes of temptation and hurt.

"Thanatos cuisine," he called it when he opened his own small kitchen. It wasn't very successful, just enough to stay open if he worked a side job. Hipsters told each other about it, and tried it…once. Other cooks came regularly to see what he was doing. He got written up in *Baltimore Magazine*. Fans crowded the restaurant every time the menu changed, and he treated them like dirt.

He dated more than ever. He liked his work. He loved watching you wince as you put the potato salad in your mouth, and screw your mouth up, and then decide to open it again—unwillingly, even though you know better. He laughed inside every time someone asked to take leftovers home.

The women who stayed with him never stayed away from his food. Once, with a tiny, big-chested girl who laughed at all his jokes, he'd tried preparing a healthy, simple salad with sweet peppers that they could eat together. But she'd seen he was preparing a truly danger-ous dirty rice on the stove and swooned at him until he fed her a spoonful. She demanded more, and threw his steel kitchenware at him when he said no. So he told her: go ahead, eat your heart out.

He'd been thinking of buying her a ring, but when she got out of the hospital it was over.

After that, he never tried to protect people from them-selves.

He had turned down the reality TV show the first time the Food Network offered it him, but he took it now. He loaned his name to a very generic cookbook of very spicy foods, and a few of his more moderate dishes were turned into frozen entrees with an impossibly hot sauce on the side. A venture capital firm offered to bankroll a chain restaurant but he wouldn't take the meetings. The money was nice, but he was in it for the thanatos, and his frozen entrees had taught him that when you make self-destruction generic you end up with McDonald's—a slow loss of standards and nutrition that eventually slides towards a heart attack. That's something, but it's not the spectacular heat or icy spike of a suicidal gesture. People who wanted to eat commercial grease until their cholesterol popped their heads in 20 years could do that, he got it, but he had no interest in making people numb.

Twelve years in, he'd gone through three sous chefs— they were such spectacular flameouts he had their pictures on the wall of his restaurant.

Thirteen years in, he married the sister of his second assistant. She was a beautiful ebony woman who worked long hours in a community violence program trying to help kids leave gangs. She owned guns, beautifully crafted guns, and knew how to shoot them. He offered to cook for her on their third date and she laughed in his face. "How about I make you a salad?" she said, and she made it with sweet peppers and a light oil. The one time they fought over whether she should even try his professional cooking, she told him, "Honey, if I was like that I'd have been dead by 20." He never asked again. As long as he kept his restaurant prices too high for poor people, she didn't mind what he did for living—but their wedding was catered.

Feeding Time

THE HOMELESS GUY ASKS US FOR MONEY SO HE CAN buy a sandwich, says he hasn't eaten in days, and Jay says "C'mon, man, if you want booze just tell us you want to buy booze"—Jay likes to think he's a real straight talker. And the guy goes "Please. You can't let me get any hungrier." Just like that—just like there's some kind of rule that says "It is illegal for a man to get any hungrier than this." And I remember thinking, wow, that's a straight talker.

So it's a Saturday night and it's not like we have any place special to go because the best party's being thrown by Ted's ex-girlfriend and we ended up on the wrong side of that breakup, and Jay says "Okay, man, how about we buy you a sandwich. You want that? We'll buy you a sandwich, but then we get to watch you eat it so we know you were really that hungry." And Ted says that's juvenile, like making him dance for spare change or something, but I'm thinking: Hey. At least he gets fed, right?

So the old guy nods, and Ted says "Okay" and I ask where we're gonna buy this guy his sandwich. And Jay, now he's all magnanimous, he's not just gonna buy him a dog from a street cart, uh uh, he says we'll go up two blocks and over one to the gourmet sub shop that's open late and we'll get this guy anything he wants off the menu.

45

Says it like he's buying him a fucking house…I mean: Come on. It's just an overpriced sandwich. Set you back ten dollars on a drinking night. Shit. That's what you get an attitude about?

So we start walking up the block, and I'm already kinda pissed about this because the corner of Alexander and East has bars everywhere and the crowds are big and there's a lot of sweet University of Rochester girls and here we are walking around with this dirty old homeless guy, we're getting all the wrong kind of looks. So the point is, Yeah. I wasn't paying attention to a word the guy said when he started to mumble, because I'm thinking I could be getting hooked up right now.

But then Ted says "Son of a bitch! Did you hear what he just said?" And James says what? And Ted says the old guy just perfectly articulated the Reimann Hypothesis. And I ask what that is, and Ted tells me to shut up because the old guy's still talking. And it sounds like gibberish to me, I don't think he's even saying words, and it turns out I'm right because Ted says he just gave the formula for Boltzman's Transport Equation. Which I think I studied in high school, but I don't remember what it is, but Ted's in the sciences, makes big money at a research lab. And now Ted's just getting really excited as the old guy keeps mumbling and he's not even checking to see if we're paying attention and we weren't but now we are. And I guess it's okay because, by that point, we'd passed all the good bars and hopefully no one remembered us.

Next is Ernst Mach's Wave Equation, which sounds impressive and Ted said he got right, and then the old guy looks around at all of us and says "I'm so hungry. It's been so long."

"Where did you learn all that?" James asks, and Ted is suddenly all into this and told the guy if he could give us more good science we'd give him a bag of chips, too. Hell, give him another sandwich.

And I ask: "Right. What's your story?" But I didn't offer any food with it, so he doesn't answer me.

Instead he starts going off on some other stuff, and I read Ted's copy of "The Elegant Universe," so I get that he's talking about quantum physics string theory stuff, and at first I'm thinking: Okay. He read the book, too. But then he starts hitting the math and Ted just freaks. And James tells him to calm down, dude, but Ted's just "Shut up!" and starts chiming in like he's in church: "Uh huh… That's right…Yes!" And James is telling him "Dude, man, calm down," but Ted's saying "Do you know how advanced this is? There's a chapter in my thesis on this part!" and won't let anybody talk.

And I'm thinking: Geez. What's this guy's story? How does he know this shit? How did his old clothes get so worn and why hasn't he shaved in…forever? Because people who know this stuff don't…well, you know. And nobody who's that scruffy poor ever gets a chance to learn anything. I'm not that kind of math guy, but Ted is and now James is totally into it, he thinks we've got the world's smartest hobo or something, like that's something to be proud of, he's such an ass sometimes, he didn't even want custody of his son and the rest of us were going: James. Come on. It's your kid, man.

So we burst into the sandwich shop and Ted doesn't even want to give him his food yet, he's all "wait, what about the square root of pi?" or something but James is saying "No, no, man, he gets a sandwich." And then Ted remembers his promise and just tells the guy behind the counter, who would have so kicked us all out if three of us didn't look like money, to give this guy anything he wants and so the homeless man just points to stuff on the menu and gets like five sandwiches, the meatiest ones they've got, like one has meatballs and the other's some kind of Italian club and one's got chicken and avocado and stuff and he starts ripping open a package of kettle cooked chips while the sandwiches are being made and Ted gets him a Mountain Dew and he sits at a table like it's the first time he's sat down in his life and shoves everything into his mouth.

Ted wants to keep talking science but this guy's a serious eater and by the time the first sandwich comes there's already crumbs all over his beard and he's not stopping. He rips into that sandwich and I think I see him wince because his teeth are bad but he just keeps going. And James is saying how sad it is that we don't have a camcorder to record this on but he takes out his cell phone and starts recording it even though he keeps complaining that the picture quality is going to suck and he should have splurged on the phone with the high resolution.

For like 20 minutes straight this guy's just packing it in, and it's obvious his mouth is in pain and his stomach hurts but he just isn't going to stop and he's finished three sandwiches and is working on a fourth when Ted starts saying we'll buy you whatever more you want if you just start talking again, because I want the good stuff. Everybody in the place is just watching us.

And the homeless guy raises the second half of the fourth sandwich up to his mouth and that's when the shaking starts. His whole body starts shaking, like epilepsy all over, and he's fighting with himself, still trying to raise the sandwich to his mouth to take another bite, but he can't because he's trembling so bad and then his fingers go crazy and he drops it, and there's tomato and salami and roast beef all over the floor and he lets out this wail because he's lost it and then his face goes pale and he doubles over and falls off the chair and is just shaking all over on the floor.

And Ted's shouting "What's wrong? What's wrong?" and James is still recording this, the fucker, and I'm thinking "Jesus, maybe he really hasn't eaten in that long." And, seriously, none of us even thinks to call an ambulance, we were just all so caught up in it because… It was the sandwich jockey behind the counter who called the hospital but this was downtown on a Saturday night and traffic was hell and there was no place for cars to get out of the way and I guess there was already a bad accident on the inner loop and it took them maybe 20 minutes to get there and after the first 10 minutes… well, he just stopped trembling.

He just stopped.

I don't know if he was dead on arrival or he died in the ambulance, but we didn't try to do CPR or anything, we didn't know what to do and touching him was—I'm not proud, okay?

He's still a John Doe. Nobody's claiming him, and his fingerprints and dental records aren't on file, or something. Nobody knows. Nobody knows what happened, and I'm not sure where we went wrong.

Should we not have fed him?

Childhoods on Display in Boston

THE DOOR OPENS AND THE BELL STRIKES. IT'S A real bell, a mechanism made by hand in 1938 and bought at a consignment store off the Boston Commons in 1981, two weeks before my shop opened. I've been more than 30 years now in the same location and still using the same bell. There isn't a computer on the premises—except for the phones people walk in with.

The walls are a giant card catalogue. It's the kind no one sees anymore. You search by name or subject or keyword and find a description written out by hand on yellowing index cards. Maybe a sample passage or two. Certainly it could be automated, but that's not in the spirit of the thing. And believe me, it makes browsing far more intense. I'm selling intimacy, after a fashion, and there's nothing more intimate than contact, running your hands over the card, smelling the ink that contains a stranger's secrets.

She has brown hair. That's the first thing I notice. She has brown hair and fair skin and hard eyes. She's wearing clothes that are stylish without being attractive. I can tell by the way her lips keep closed that if she were to smile I'd like it. But she's not smiling.

She walks over the wooden floor on shoes that have very small heels. I smile politely. There is a decorum among shopkeepers, passed down through generations. It's a lost art today, but I sell lost arts, in a manner of speaking. "How may I help you?"

Like many people visiting for the first time, she doesn't know exactly where she is. "You sell...?"

"Childhoods," I say. "Yes."

Her face drops. I can see the metaphor will only cause confusion.

"Diaries, Miss," although she's really a ma'am. "I sell diaries. Mostly of children and adolescents, but some adults."

She nods.

"They are indexed, alphabetized, and catalogued by subject area. I can find you any kind of life you want to read."

She looks around but sees only the card catalogue. I can see that she's looking for something to focus on that will make the exchange more ordinary.

"My therapist told me about you," she says.

"I get a number of referrals. I should point out that insurance doesn't cover purchases made here."

"No," she says. "No."

"Is there something I can help you find?" I ask. "What kind of life are you looking for?"

She looks around again. Of course none of my wares are on display for perusal. They're historical documents, easily damaged.

We're alone in the store but she leans over to whisper anyway. "Embarrassing moments."

"Ah." I smile reassuringly. "We'll be able to help you, then. My collection is extensive. Is there anything in particular you're looking for?"

"I'm ..." she begins, and then she stops. She doesn't like being here. Her features harden and her spine stiffens. She doesn't know how to do this gracefully.

Her face contorts. I expect she's used to giving orders, not asking for help. Wherever she is, she's the boss. I know it. She has employees. She tells them what to do. She's wearing a ring, so perhaps she's married. I'm sure she's the partner who makes the decisions.

"When I was twelve," she tells me, loudly now, so that if someone else were in the shop they'd be sure to overhear, "I was on an airplane going to see my grandparents, and I went to the bathroom in the front of the plane, and I pulled up my dress and pulled down my panties, and just as I was sitting down—I hadn't shut the door correctly, so it opened up and I flashed the entire airplane, and everybody was looking."

Her features stay hard but her face is flushed. Her chest, what little I can see of it, is red too. "It was three more hours on the flight, and I had to get up and close the door, and then walk back down the row, and sit down next to people. I almost died."

"You seem to have done fine," I say.

"I ..." she steels herself. Am I really that unpleasant to talk to? Most people seem to enjoy confiding in me. "I've never gotten over it. I don't know how to."

"Ah."

"I know it's not the worst thing in the world," she says.

"It's not," I agree.

"But I keep thinking about it."

"I understand. May I…"

"I'm looking for diaries of other people's embarrassing… shameful…moments like that. And how they got over it."

"Of course," I say. I gesture to the east catalogue. "May I introduce you to our lost virginity section? The entries with the black dots indicate trauma—the girls who were taken by surprise, who were laughed at, who were caught by older children in a remote location. Look through, see what appeals to you. In the meantime I'll bring up the notebooks of a Miss D., who was tricked into performing in front of her brother, and a Miss S., who had her dress pulled up during a middle school play. I believe you'll find that one most helpful."

She stares at me and her eyes narrow. "You have…this entire collection memorized, don't you?"

I nod. "It helps to provide exceptional service."

"You've read every one?"

I take a deep breath. "I think of myself as a curator."

"Of what?"

"Of human experience. In a manner of speaking."

Her mouth twists, and it's easy to see what she thinks of me.

"Do you keep a diary?" she asks.

"I do not have that gift."

She nods. I can see it's the one thing we have in common. I show her to the catalogue, and then step away into the locked room to retrieve the manuscripts. The diaries are kept in sealed plastic slips. The set I'm looking for consists of a leather-bound volume with gold-tipped pages and a spiral-bound notebook written in red pen. Poor Miss S. Her mother sold me the work in 1996 and I have kept it better than they kept her. The essences contained in private moments are a kind of psychological stem cell, capable of becoming whatever emotional organs they need to be for other people. I have seen the transformation many times. But you need to harvest them somewhere. And only another person's memories will serve. If my newest customer had written down her experience on the plane and let it sit for decades maturing like a child or a fine wine, it would be a balm for the sickness of someone else's soul. Provided by my curatorial hands.

I remove the diaries from their cases and take them out to my waiting customer, who is handling my catalogue through gloves. I resent her judgment, but I am dedicated to service, and we're going to get this right.

The Fix

I DIDN'T EAT ALL DAY SO THAT I COULD FIT INTO THE leather skirt. The pale sweater clung to my skin like whipped cream. I'd bought the right shade of lipstick just for tonight. It looked like blood and tasted like stale milk. I'd never wear it again.

Deciding that I had to do it was the hardest part: I'd never thought of myself as that kind of girl. And if I was going to do it, it had to be done right.

I put on the highest heels I had, open-toed pumps that turned my legs into elegant works of art. My ass was a beacon. I put a chain with a silver skull around my ankle. It was a gift from my sister Jesse, who I think had found it on the floor after her wedding. Nothing about that had made sense.

I just needed one more thing. The bolt cutters were on the kitchen counter, picked up fresh from Wal-Mart today. As heavy as they looked. I picked them up and snapped them a few times in the air, just to feel it.

I picked up my keys and got in the truck. My housemate Stacey was out for the night, so getting out of the driveway was easy. I put my foot on the gas and kept it there.

40 Caliber is not a nice bar, although it's worse on a Saturday than a Thursday. Thursdays are just a three-

fight night. Rubes park in the front, regulars in the back. I drove the truck around back and left it running, because I didn't belong. I knew this would have to be quick.

The lot was empty. Jason's bike was in its usual spot. If someone had been there I would have done exactly what I did, only with them watching me—and maybe I would have felt more powerful, or maybe I would have been terrified. But I had dressed up, and I still would have done it.

The juke box inside was playing something nasty and the parking lot light was flickering as I got out of the truck and opened the bed. I lowered the detachable ramp. I walked over to the bike, my heels clacking on the blacktop, and hefted the bolt cutters. I snapped the anti-theft device in two. I put the key he didn't know I had copied months ago in the ignition, and pushed. Once it was in the bed I tipped it on its side—that's all the protection it needed—and detached the ramp and closed the back.

I got back in the truck and drove away. So easy. I drove along the lake for a while, just because I could. At the right stretch of road the Chicago skyline looks like something in a pop-up book, as though it hadn't been there a moment ago and won't be there a moment later when you turn the page.

I was at Hermano's by 10:30. The shop was closed but he was waiting for me. He whistled twice, once when he saw me in my one-night-only outfit and again when he saw the bike. We rolled it out and he replaced the wheels and swapped out the handle bars and mirrors and painted it pink and white. Then we loaded it back up on the truck and I drove away.

I was at the Klassy Kat Lounge by 1:00. I got in free because they don't charge women, and sat in a booth drinking a ginger ale and looking unapproachable until Lilly had finished her set. I got lipstick all over the glass. Then I waved her over.

"Wow," she said. "Look at you!"

"Come out back," I told her. She went and got a robe and then we walked out into the parking lot.

"How are you holding up?" she asked me.

"You got it worse than I did," I told her. "That's why I wanted to do something for you. For us both, really, but you most of all."

"He's leprosy on two legs with a small dick who hangs on to his mom's teat with his only good teeth because he can't pay a bill on his own," she said. "Fuck."

We got to my truck and I opened the bed, released the catch, and wheeled the motorcycle back down.

She didn't recognize it for a moment, a girly motorcycle glowing in the parking lot.

"Oh my…" she gaped. " Oh my…holy shit…that's not…is that?"

I held out the key. She started laughing. "Ohmygod, ohmygod, ohmygod."

"It's yours," I said. "You'll have to get your own fake papers…sorry about that…I don't know how to do that, but, I hope you drive it around. It gets great gas mileage. It feels great between…well, you know." She was still laughing. She grabbed the keys. She grabbed me. She tried to make out with me, but, I'm not like that.

"God I love you right now," she said. And I hugged her

59

because I think I knew how she meant it.

"He had it coming," I said. "He so had this..."

She started laughing again and we agreed to get together sometime. I got in my truck, smiling like the queen of the world, and drove back home. I put the radio on and rolled the windows down and sang along.

Stacey was back. It was hard to get into my spot. I opened the door and saw her there with her sister Amanda. They saw me and their jaws dropped and Stacey started laughing. I walked inside like it was my personal runway. Then I couldn't take it anymore.

I kicked the shoes off. Those fucking shoes. There was a fire going, so I picked the shoes up by their heels and walked over to the fireplace and threw them in. They started to melt and it smelled terrible.

"What the fuck?" Stacey said.

I slipped the skirt off, right in front of them. "I'm getting rid of these clothes," I said. "I have to. I'm not this person really, I can't...I can't go back here too often. It's like...I'm so amoral right now."

"What did you do?"

"I made the world a better place."

Amanda said "You're a goddess!"

The sweater and skirt both went in the fire. The spirit started to vanish. "I'll..." I stared at them. "I'll...burn the underwear in a minute," I said, and started to walk to my room.

"Wait!" Amanda shouted to my back.

I stopped and turned.

"Can I..." Amanda hesitated. "Can I have the anklet?"

"What?" I'd forgotten all about it. "I…I…what do you want to do with it?"

"I don't know," she said softly. She was so young, I realized, and I was still in my 20s. "But I…if you're going to destroy it anyway…I think I want to keep part of this. Whatever it is. Can I…?"

I bent down and unpinned it. I walked over and handed it to her and then ran back to my room, suddenly wiped out. Hungry for new dreams.

I stopped thinking about Jason the next day, and soon I barely remembered him. I saw Lilly riding around on that bike all the time—it was great. Once a friend of mine said "Do you know Jason thinks you stole his bike? He's gone, like crazy paranoid." And I knew I'd won. I'd fixed it.

I haven't seen Stacey much over the last few years…I think maybe I've seen Amanda once. I don't know what happened to the anklet. I didn't ask. But I like to think it makes its way from hand to hand, and that there's a goddess inside who can do what needs to be done.

Memoir

THE OLD MAN PICKS UP A CRYSTAL IN THE SHAPE OF a cone. The inside of it is foggy; his fingers are wrinkled and shaking. He holds it out as though showing me a rare coin. The workshop smells of jasmine and Creole cooking.

"This," he says, "is the day you ran away from home but stopped because for a moment you saw the structure of the universe in the space between the leaves on a tree. You sat watching them sway, and knew perfect joy." He peers closely at the crystal cone, squinting his eyes. "Then you began to laugh. For half an hour, I'd say, you laughed. And then you went back, because you knew it would be all right."

He puts the cone back down on the black velvet cloth behind him and raises his fading eyebrows. "Has everything turned out all right?"

That's not a fair question. I shake my head. They warned me he was difficult to work with. "Not it," I say.

"Not it," he repeats, annoyed. He reaches behind him and picks up another crystal, a little larger than his hand, the shape of a rectangular box. The fog inside is a different color. "You were older this time," he says. "Years have passed. You were the lead in the high school play, yes? They picked the show just for you, and when you strode across the stage for the curtain call you were lightning and the applause was thunder. I don't know the play. I don't keep up with the theater. But you were wearing a suit, and for all the times you'd said you were the center of the universe, this was the first time you really believed it."

"Not it." I shake my head. School play? Please.

"Not it," he says, and puts the crystal back. "It would help if you could be more specific."

"I'll know it when I see it."

He sighs and looks back at the small row of crystal shapes displayed on black velvet, under the light of a single oil lamp. "I notice," he says, "that there are very few moments of such intense joy in your life."

I lean forward. "That's why we should be able to find it, isn't it."

He leans back. His breath smells of garlic and onions. His tongue is covered in flecks of spit. The bayou spits out ugly old men. "I only suggest that perhaps what you need is a therapist."

"And yet I'm here."

He nods. "And yet you are. Perhaps the reason that you won't tell me what I'm looking for is because you don't know?"

"Or it's something I don't want to talk about." I reach into my pocket and take out 10 hundred-dollar bills. I slide them across the table. "I'm private."

If he liked me I wouldn't have to bribe him. He picks up each bill one by one, folds each one carefully and puts each one in his coat pocket. He reaches behind him and

64

takes a crystal in his hand. A perfect sphere, a crystal ball, filled with dark fog.

"More malice in this one," he says. "You defeated some-one. Gave him a bloody nose in a dark alley behind a college dorm, with people watching...people who had expected you to be the one on the ground, swearing. You surprised them all and you won. And you liked it so much."

Ah yes. I remember.

"Not it," I say. But I'm less annoyed. I still like to win.

He scowls. He shakes his head. "This usually doesn't take so long."

I nod. "It's lucky I'm not a happy man."

He picks up a small cup of steaming green tea. He blows on it softly and puts it to his lips.

"Try again."

He drains the cup. "Ah," he says. He smacks his lips and puts the cup away. He reaches behind him and grabs a crystal square. He looks at it.

"Sex," he says simply. "The first time that you tied her down and it worked. It made..."

"Not it."

He looks up, surprised. "Not it?"

"Move on."

He shakes his head, reluctant to put the crystal down. "This would have made sense."

"Not it."

"All right." He holds it for a moment longer. Stop look-ing at her, old man. "Was she...?" he starts to ask, and I put my hand between his eyes and the cube. His head snaps up. He stares, he sees the look in my eyes, and I'm sure he saw what he shouldn't have. If he pretends not to, we can go on. He opens his mouth.

"Of course," he says, and he puts the cube away, careful not to look at it again. His hands are shaking more now.

"Move on."

He doesn't say anything. He picks up a crystal sliver, the size of a toothpick. "This..." he blinks, stares, his mouth tightens. "I don't...understand...this makes no sense. How is...what happened to her?"

"That's it." I hold my hand out. "Give it to me."

He doesn't move. His eyes are fixed. When I lean in to block his view he leans back and withdraws his arm.

"You can't have. Impossible."

He stares at me as though the world is falling apart over my shoulder.

"This...is a moment of intense joy for you!" he says.

He probably shouldn't have said that. I tilt my head, a very slight shrug. "You don't understand. Leave it at that. Let's finish this up and call it a day."

He looks back at the crystal. "She's calling for help."

"Yes, she was." I make an invitation with my fingers for him to put it in my hand. "I'm the help."

He looks back at it, stares, wastes precious time. "No, you're not..."

"It's my memory, I'm the authority here. Finish our business."

He leans back again, as far away as his back can bend. He looks at me, and back at the crystal, so small, so delicate. "I can't just leave her..."

66

My eyes narrow. I was afraid something like this might happen. "She's just a memory, old man. You know that."

He's lost. She's always had that effect on people.

"What kind of man would I be," he asks, "if I abandoned her for…business?"

I nod. I take my hand back. "That's a very good question, very near to my heart." I reach under my coat, pull out my gun and shoot him. With a silencer. There's barely a ping.

He collapses, falls off his chair, falls under the row of crystals…my memories.

Well, what did he think was going to happen? He knows I like to win.

I stand up and walk back around the table. I stand over the body. Am I really going to offer some home-spun wisdom over his corpse? Really? I shake my head, put my gun back in its holster and kneel down. I take the small crystal in my thumb and forefinger.

He was right. I can hear her. I lean closer. "Hello, beautiful. You almost got away this time."

I can't hear what she says, but there's time for that later. Besides, she always says the same thing, really— except that as I change my memory changes too, which is where this gets interesting. Memories are living things: they evolve and adapt. They're capable of supporting life.

I put the tiny crystal in my shirt pocket, where I keep nothing else, and stand up. Upon consideration, I grab the other crystals on the velvet cloth and stuff them where I can. Leaving them behind is a bad idea. I'm not worried about fingerprints…there's no chance his people are going to the police...but leaving them is just asking for trouble.

Motion catches my eye—on a small shelf nearby holding empty crystals, smoke like a thundercloud streaked with silver has just filled a small pyramid.

How does that work? Was this an intensely joyful moment for me? No, that couldn't be. Maybe something's gone wrong now that the old man's dead. That makes more sense.

Or maybe this is joyful.

Really, what do I know about what makes people happy?

I blow out the oil lamp and slip away.

Some of the
Social Issues
Surrounding Jazz

THERE'S NO ONE IN THE AUDIENCE BUT ME AND THE club is dark so maybe he doesn't know that. He adjusts his tie before he steps up to the microphone. I sit at a rickety table in the third row, probably just out of his range of vision under the heavy lights. I'm drinking a New Orleans-style hurricane, and the ice plinks in the glass because my hand isn't steady. He clears his throat so that he can speak clearly.

"Hello, and thank you for coming," he says. "I would like to welcome everyone to this month's Conversations on Jazz." Maybe he doesn't know.

Who am I kidding? He knows.

His black skin reflects. His bald head is sweating. His hands are unsteady like mine, but for him it's age rather than the drink. He comes to talk about the history of jazz every month on the one night the club has no music. Last night was hip-hop. Tomorrow will be metal. The club's owner is a friend of his from back in the day, a fellow musician, I think. I'm the only person in the audience, ever. Of course he knows.

"Mostly these talks deal with contemporary aspects of the music itself," he says, "new trends in instrumentation or the makeup of ensembles. But tonight I thought we would move in a slightly different direction and talk about some of the social issues surrounding jazz."

His delivery is formal, his voice unwavering. Not once has he ever acknowledged that no one's listening. Not once have I seen him look tired of the charade.

"There are a variety of social forces that have been transforming jazz music, first in its present incarnation, but even more perniciously, revising its history as well—not to correct errors but to make it look like jazz's more bland, innocuous present. I will begin with the first of those impacts and move on to the second."

Maybe he's my hero or maybe I'm just waiting for him to crack. Both would be like me.

"For all that jazz's popularity with a mass audience is declining, its standing as an academic subject has never been higher. There are now dozens of graduate-level programs in jazz music at schools across the country, which seems like it would be good for the music—but who do they find to teach them? Most of the working jazz musicians with ties to the club and bar scene lack the proper credentials for academic institutions, and so instead academics are selected for faculty. Yet since virtually all of these faculty members lack ties to the clubs and bars that have made up jazz's traditional home—I don't think it is an exaggeration to say that most of them have never been working musicians in their lives—they have absolutely no personal connection to the methods by which jazz's history and institutional knowledge have been transmitted from generation to generation."

My drink is done and the waitress plunks another on my table before I even signal. It's the only sound to come from the audience.

"Naturally this is having an effect on the kind of music that emerges today, especially since record executives who do not know their asses from their elbows go to the academies of music instead of the club scene to find potential recording artists. Jazz music as represented by record companies is now drawn primarily from white institutions, and you cannot ignore the impact that has. The emergence of so-called smooth jazz as a major category of music, for example—what is that? What is "smooth jazz" but music made more palatable for people who do not really want to listen? Jazz as most people hear it today is more a creation of white academia than working black musicians."

I nod. Over and over again. Then I drink. Sweat from his forehead drips down the side of his face. It doesn't go near his eyes. His eyes stare out into the darkness trying to focus on what he knows isn't there. If he looks at me, ever, I don't see it.

"But what is even more pernicious is the way jazz's co-option by white record companies is affecting the recollection of its history. Once again, the fact that virtually no jazz teachers at the graduate level have ever been working musicians is having an enormous effect, since jazz history was traditionally passed down through the club scene, by working with the musicians who worked with the musicians.

Take that away and there is nothing to replace the oral history."

Tell it, brother. Tell it. I scoop up a handful of bar peanuts from the bowl they know to put down on the table when I come in.

I spill them; they clatter as they fall over everything.

Tell it.

"Working jazz musicians formed a small and tightly knit society, and plagiarism, for example, was prevented because everyone knew who had made each innovation and would not let you get away with performing in that style without giving credit. Honesty was enforced and individuality encouraged. You had to be original to make your mark."

I take a long drink, and wince. That's stronger than usual.

"But with the institutions that study jazz disconnected from that collective knowledge, it is easy for the history to be rewritten to suit modern prejudices. I recently heard an argument in which a jazz professor at a respected institution here in Chicago said that Stan Getz had influenced Lester Young."

I hiss.

"This is nonsense. Of course it was the other way around, you just have to look at the chronology to see that. We—the musicians who made up their peers—we knew that. But now we see prominent so-called experts, from positions of power, rewriting history, and it is no accident that the safer, white musician is given the credit as the leader and innovator."

No one walks through the door, but he goes on. Drink after drink is delivered to me—I think it's my tab that keeps the owner ready to leave the place open the last Monday of every month—while he goes on, moving from the musicians I have in my collection to names I've never heard of. I'd think he was making some of them up, but I have absolute confidence in his honesty. Look at his face: somehow he stares right into the bright stage lights and doesn't blink.

I once saw a portrait of Bernard Clairveaux, the 12th century saint who was so sure God ordained the conquest of the Holy Land that he gathered up an army of children and sent them off to war in the desert. It's the same look, except what this man saw, back in the day when a trumpet player could hitchhike from city to city and step in with bands who already knew his name and sound and be part of something good—what this man saw was real.

Now it's gone. Just like the children.

Maybe it wasn't Clairveaux's portrait I saw. I'm drunk now, but I'm a quiet drunk, so he can go on, he can go on, he can go on. Maybe it was someone else. The Children's Crusade didn't go well. Crusades never go well. But I am here, dizzy and sweating, my tongue sweet and salty and on fire, unable to speak.

So when he comes to the end of his speech and asks, "Are there any questions?" there is silence.

Just the clinking of ice in my glass and peanuts falling off the table, and that could mean anything.

He thanks us all for coming. He hopes we'll all come

back next month.

He walks off the stage and doesn't look at me. Or maybe the lights are too bright and he can't see anything as he walks out of the club.

He knows. Of course he knows.

Elijah Drinks Chimay

IT'S A BAR DISGUISED AS AN ART GALLERY BUT THAT'S okay, I like both. Light techno music ka-thump-thidda-thumps over loudspeakers and the bright sun shines through big windows. I'd have preferred someplace darker (the West Coast is so bright) but it's time to sit down. I've been walking all day.

The art's no good—black-and-white photographs of naked forms that scream, "My senior thesis is meant to be shocking." But if the beer's all right it's a worthy sacrifice.

That's true of so many things. I sit at the bar in the center of the cavernous room and look over the liquors. There's an attractive woman sitting a few stools down.

This place has everything but a bartender. No sign of him.

But I can wait. I've got impressions to sort through, a city to judge.

I like the temperature—cool and pleasant. Warm temperatures attract stupid people; chill brings out the best in human nature. But that's just one of many factors I have to consider. It's my first time in San Francisco and, despite its reputation, I haven't decided yet whether the city is worthy of me.

Is that arrogant? Sure. But it's a decision we all make at some point—and if you're going to have standards at all, why not have high ones?

It's amazing how often I have to explain this to people.

I try to make eye contact with the woman a few seats down, but she's talking on her cell phone.

"Yeah," she says, "no, I was there last night. I think it starts at 11." She doesn't look my way. All for the best.

A tall, sandy-haired white man, fit but a little puffy around the face, walks behind the bar and over to me.

"Yes?" he asks.

His hair is really sand colored. I can't get over that—like it grew out of a beach.

"Can I help you?" he asks. He has a light accent. European? I can almost place it.

"Yeah," I say. And then I shake my head. "Yeah," I say again, and this time I mean it. Time to test the local mettle. "Got any Belgian beers?"

"Yes," he says. "We have Stella on tap."

"No, no, no," I say. "That's the Budweiser of Belgium."

His lips twitch a little. "Yes," he says.

"How about ales?" I ask. "I'm particularly fond of the Trappist ales."

"We have Chimay," he says.

"Ah," I say. "Very good."

"Yes," he says.

"Some would say the best beer in the world."

"Yes," he says.

"I am among them."

"Yes, it's a good choice," he says. "Would you like one?"

"Yes I—wait."

He does.

"Do you have the red, the white or the blue label?"

"Red and blue," he says.

I smile. "Excellent."

He nods. "I was afraid you were going to say the white was your favorite."

I scowl. "The white is the only one I'm not fond of."

"Me too," he says. "Which would you like?"

"I'd like a blue, please."

He turns around and reaches down to a lower shelf and pulls out a small bottle of Chimay blue label. He walks over to another shelf and pulls a glass...the appropriately shaped glass...with the Abbey label on it, no less...and makes a perfect pour.

I nod. "You've even got the right glasses," I say as he sets it in front of me. "I didn't expect that."

He shrugs.

I pick the glass up and take a sip. I have a weakness for this beer, and it shows on my face. He watches me drink.

"You know, it's especially good just lightly aged," I say.

"I've had it like that," he agrees.

"I've actually traveled to the monastery in Belgium where the monks make it," I say.

"Me too," he says.

I raise my eyebrows. "Really?"

He nods. "I'm Belgian. I grew up about a half-hour away from The Abbey de Scourmont."

I consider this for a moment, and then extend my hand.

He takes it. "I'm Martin," he says, with the last syllable stressed.

"Elijah," I say.

"E..." he looks taken aback.

"It's a pleasure to meet you, Martin. You don't know how great a pleasure."

"Elijah," he says, pronouncing every syllable separately.

I take another sip. Heaven. "I've been walking all over this city. And do you know what? You're the first person I've really liked."

"Like the prophet?" he asks.

"Like the prophet."

"Who blows his horn at the end?"

"Of the world. Yes. I've got to tell you something about this city, Martin. You've got an amazing park here. Golden Gate Park is easily the best park I've seen outside of the one in Paris...what's its name...the one with the City of Science in it, and the big geode..."

"The Parc de la Villette."

"Yeah. That's the one. But this? Easily Number 2."

"Can I tell you..." he says, then stops.

"I'm new in town, I'm thinking of living here, and that park makes me love this city. But...well..."

"You look just like a painting I once saw." He's staring straight at me.

"You mean a character in a painting?"

"Yes. Of the prophet Elijah. It's very...uncanny."

I nod. "One of the Renaissance paintings?"

"Yes."

"Are you a Catholic, Martin?"

"Yes."

"Of course you are. I love you guys." I take a long drink.

"The Prophet Elijah with Book," he says. "That was it."

"By Pier Francesco Mola. Yeah, I know the one."

"Except that you look younger. But it's unmistakable."

"I guess so. Can I run some thoughts about this city by you?"

"I…" He blinks, pauses, and then leans forward. "Of course."

I nod and open my mouth.

He interrupts. "But first…I must know."

"Yes?"

"Are you the prophet Elijah, who was taken bodily up to heaven by God?"

I wave that away. "Of course not."

"If I may say…You don't seem surprised by the question."

"Nah. It's not the first time."

"Really?"

"Yeah. Now the Asian food here is really good, too, except the sushi's overrated. There are a few small fish marts that are everything they're supposed to be. But I've got to tell you, there's something that really bothers me about this city, and I've just put my finger on it."

"Okay."

"Are you familiar with the American sociologist Charles Rieff?"

"No. Wait…You mean Philip Rieff?"

I snap my fingers. "Right. That's his name."

"Would you like another beer?" He's already moving to the cabinet to pull out another blue bottle.

"Yes."

"It's on the house." He makes another perfect pour.

"That's not because you think I'm the keeper of the Horn of Doom, is it?"

"No. It's for the conversation."

"Thanks. Now, Philip Rieff coined the term 'Therapeutic Society.' He didn't mean it as a compliment…you must know that…and that's what keeps running through my mind when I think of San Francisco." I pause to take a sip of my beer, catch the head while it's still bubbly.

"A Therapeutic Society?"

I sit back on my barstool. I swirl the rich foaming liquid around my mouth, over my tongue. Little pleasures. "Yeah. A society more interested in expressing what it believes than in actually believing anything. A society more interested in confessing what it's done than in actually doing anything. A society in which communication-of-self replaces thought, morality, and action. Every institution is eventually co-opted to assist in this navel gazing. The whole society dedicates itself to producing not men, but 'therapeutic man.'" I take another sip.

"Therapeutic man," he says.

"Another of Rieff's terms."

"Yes—although I think it was 'Psychological Man.'"

I shrug. "Either way, it refers to a person who thinks that how he feels about something is more important than the thing itself."

"This is an old complaint," says Martin. "You're talking about relativism."

"No—I'm talking about narcissism, and a society that treats life as though it were a therapist's couch."

The woman a few seats down is waving to get his attention.

"Excuse me," he says.

"Chocolate martini," she says.

"You should meet my friend," Martin tells her. "He's very interesting."

She turns to look at me for the first time. Her gaze is piercing. I can't tell what color her hair is because with the sun shining on her through the skylight she's blond, but when she leans forward out of the light, her hair is black. Her blouse is green. She extends her hand. I extend mine.

Her hands are cold. Her grip is strong.

"Lilith," she says.

I chuckle. Of course. "Elijah."

Her eyebrows rise. "Eli...really?"

"Very."

She moves two stools closer. She crosses her legs. She's wearing a short skirt and high boots. On other women it would look like trying too hard, but she pulls it off.

She tilts her head. "This reminds me of a story," she says.

"I like stories."

"I read it a long time ago. It was a medieval monk. He was being tempted by a demoness. Every night she would come to him and try to tempt him with her succulent flesh...and in response he would preach to her about the glory of God."

Martin sets the drink down before her, leans against the counter and listens.

"Night after night, week after week, month after month, the demoness would come to him at night to tempt him with her body and he would preach to her about the light of God. Then one day he decided he could not take it anymore and would yield to her charms. He waited all day. He stripped his body naked and that night she appeared. She was clothed in chaste robes. She had pledged her life to God. I haven't thought about that story in years."

"It's by Anatole France," I say.

"Didn't he also write the one about the juggler who performs before the statue of the Virgin Mary?" asks Martin. "And after he collapses she wipes his brow?"

"Yeah."

"That story made me cry," says Lilith.

"Which one? The story about the juggler, or the story about the monk and the demoness?"

"The juggler," she says. "The one about the monk made me laugh."

Martin shakes his head, but I disagree. "Laughter is always an appropriate reaction."

She runs a finger around the rim of her glass. "Are you a monk?"

"No."

"He's drinking beer made by monks," Martin offers. "He knows it's the best in the world."

She purses her lips. "Are you a demon?"

"No."

"He's a prophet," says Martin. "Elijah was just telling me why he doesn't like San Francisco."

Her eyes widen. "You're kidding."

"It's true," he says.

"I've never met anyone who doesn't like San Francisco. Are you paranoid about earthquakes?"

I shake my head. "No."

"He will cause it," says Martin. "He is here to blow his ram's horn, the earth will shake, and San Francisco will sink into the sea, because he thinks we're self-indulgent."

She laughs. "I have to defend my favorite city," she says. "I have to keep you from drowning us all in the sea."

"You're not from around here," I say.

"No. I visit. Every chance I get."

"Why don't you stay?"

"Touché," she admits.

"It's because you'd lose your edge here. You can't stay sharp when everyone's stroking your ego. And ego stroking's exactly the problem. Martin lives here," I say, pointing at him. "And after meeting me for five minutes, he already thinks I'm a character out of the Old Testament. That should tell you something."

Martin holds up his hands. "There's a creative, entrepreneurial spirit here."

I put my glass down. "There's a pastry shop in Palestine, Gaza, that creates the most beautiful confection of honey, olives and unleavened bread. In the world there is no better dessert. It is sweet and then salty at once, and the crispy texture catches behind your teeth and melts so that the flavor lingers and expands between bites. Children line up in the street before the shop opens. Old men send their wives to pick up a bag to make the sting of age fade away while they sit and drink tea with their memories. And you stand in line, smelling the delight to come, and think, this is paradise on earth."

I take a drink. "But here's the thing. Every dollar made in that bakery is sent to a school for suicide bombers run

83

by Hamas. Two weeks ago they tried to blow up an Israeli preschool. They failed because the men they sent were too eager. Their big smiles and their heavy coats raised alarm. But that was a fluke."

Everyone's quiet.

"They've blown up bus stations, restaurants and synagogues." I finish my beer. "Take the long view, Martin. Fuck your entrepreneurial spirit."

He quietly removes my glass.

"That's a ridiculous comparison," Lilith says. "We're not murderers, Eli."

"My name's Elijah. I don't shorten it."

"We're nothing like those people."

"The point is, you have to look deeper. How can a self-styled community of artists and free thinkers get so self-indulgent?"

They look at me blankly. I sigh and look up at the ceiling. "I still haven't met anyone here more creative than the people I knew in Indianapolis—and they're all the more impressive for thriving in an apathetic environment. And if I tell people in New York City, 'There are these really creative people in the Midwest,' they say, 'Great! I should go check out that scene!' And if I tell people in London, 'Have you seen what's going on in Bristol?' they say, 'Is it good? Is there anything I can learn from it? ' But when I tell people here, 'You've got a lot to learn from what's happening in Buffalo,' they get offended. Why? Because I'm not indulging them. That vanity is revealing."

"Those are the places people came here to get away from," says Martin.

84

"And what's interesting is that they lose all respect for the people who stay behind. They turn themselves into false idols. The city's full of them. And that kind of self-indulgence is a plague."

"Maybe you'd be happier some place where people don't admit they have feelings," says Lilith.

"Where do you live, Lilith? Where are you when you don't have the chance to visit?"

"I'm in finance," she says. "I follow the markets."

"Then let me ask you something—is San Francisco a good long-term risk?"

She hesitates.

"Is it? Would you invest in real estate? Locate a new company here? Invest in a new company that's buying real estate here for the long term?"

She frowns.

"Of course not," I say. "Because San Francisco's a doomed city. Soon the sea will rise and the earth will tremble and not even the corpses of the powerful will be found."

She laughs.

"Prophet," whispers Martin.

"Common knowledge," I tell him. "It's not prophecy if it's written up in the *New York Times*."

"Your drinks are still on the house," he says.

I turn back to Lilith, whose eyes are sparkling. "This very spot we sit will be swallowed by the earth, and you know it and I know it and everyone knows it. Yet not a shred of their impending mortality has pierced the average resident's dreams."

She licks the chocolate around the rim of her martini glass. "You'd like us more if we were afraid."

"The loss of fear and respect are symptoms of what I object to."

"Why don't you go by Eli?" she asks.

I shake my head. "Some things cannot be abbreviated."

"A friend of mine likes to call 'The Dalai Lama' 'The Dalai,'" she says. "I think it's cute."

"Cute." I take a deep breath. "The words 'Dalai Lama' mean 'Ocean of Wisdom' in Tibetan. By abbreviating it, she's calling him just 'The Ocean,' which is nonsensical."

She snorts. "We all know what she's talking about."

"Perhaps you're all equally ignorant."

"I don't think the Dalai Lama would object."

"He has compassion for all sentient beings. We're not in the same line of work."

She picks up her glass in her left hand and leans back, catching her hair in the sunlight. "Okay, Elijah, tell us how we should all live."

I look back at the bar. "You see, Martin? In a Therapeutic Society, anything that doesn't make us feel good is intrinsically bad. Hence, wisdom is not possible. Virtue is not possible."

He looks at Lilith. "Rieff said that," he agrees. "Virtue gives way to value."

"And what's of value is whatever pleases us today," I nod. "Commitment to a higher ideal is impossible. Truth is a means to therapy, to be dropped when it makes us feel bad."

"People have a right to feel happy," Lilith says.

"People have a right to earn their happiness," I say.

"You get worked up over nothing" Lilith says.

"You don't think this kind of self-indulgence epitomizes the moment a culture loses the right to survive?"

"You should cut him off, Martin," Lilith says.

He shakes his head. "He was this way when he came in."

"I'm a paying customer. Do what I tell you," she tells him sweetly. "Get over yourself," she says to me softly. "What you call self-indulgence is freedom—the freedom to set your own priorities in the face of anything, to be who you want to be regardless of who disapproves. That's why I love it here: It's filled with people yielding to their inner urges, being whoever they feel driven to be."

"A Therapeutic Society," I say. "Where what you feel about something is more important than the reality of it. It always leads to the worst kind of self-indulgence."

"It leads to liberty," she shoots back. "And you moralists don't like it because we stand up to you. Get thee behind me, Elijah: You can't judge us."

I sip my beer. "No one's ever said that and lasted."

"This is the modern world," she says. "We understand that an earthquake isn't a moral judgment. That's why we have more fun. Try it sometime."

"The best beer in the world," I say, "is brewed by monks."

"I drink martinis."

"The price of liberty," I say, "is eternal vigilance, whatever you drink. That's not a choice, it's a law laid down by the Throne of Heaven." I take a breath. "Speaking metaphorically, of course. Once you give up vigilance, liberty comes crashing down around you like the Tower of Babel."

"Is that it, then?" Martin whispers. "Will you go to the seaside and sound your horn?"

"You remind me of the Aztecs," I say. "When Cortez arrived they spared his life because he looked like the God Quetzalcoatl, the Lord of Flowers, who was fated to return. And so, because of a resemblance, they let the Spanish take hold. Because of a coincidence, their civilization fell and their children were enslaved and their women raped and their land plundered and the scars remain to this day. Cortez was not Quetzalcoatl and I am not Elijah, whatever you may think."

Lilith smiles. "That's too bad," she says. "I've never met a prophet before."

"You wouldn't know how to listen if you did." I sigh. "The end of the world won't begin here, Martin. It won't need to: you're already destroying yourselves. Do you know where the end of the world is going to start?" He waits. "I shouldn't tell you this: it's going to begin someplace where everyone is too busy doing good works to think for a moment that the eyes of God are upon them. They'll never think they're that important."

He nods. "That's their bad luck."

"That's their bad luck." I get up. "Thanks for all the beer."

"Thanks for the conversation."

"You're the only man I met, in all of San Francisco, whom I liked. But that counts for something."

"This is not Sodom and Gomorrah?" he asks.

"That," I say, "is a bad comparison."

Lilith reaches out and grabs my hand. "Wait," she says. She holds out a black address book. "Sign," she says.

I take a red pen out of my pocket and write down my first name. Nothing else.

She nods. "Proof," she says, "that this really happened. No one would believe me if I just told them."

I sigh. "This is going to lead to a misunderstanding of mythic proportions."

"Complete with relic," says Martin, glancing at her address book.

I walk out the door and into the sunlight. The West Coast is too bright. There's so much more walking to do.

Rock God

REAL ROCK STARS, HERE'S THE THING, YOU WITH ME, you feeling me?

Come on, put your hand on my heart, feel it beat, that's energy from me to you. Real rock stars, it's not about the music, it's about the energy. People aren't coming to listen to music, they aren't coming to a concert—a thing, a noun. Get it? They're coming to ROCK—a verb, an action: a rock star is a shaman leading his people into a trance state, giving them the power they seek.

Yeah, keep your hand there.

You an Israeli? You sound Israeli. I guess anyone who speaks fluent Hebrew sounds Israeli. It's that kind of country, babe. No, keep your hand there. Me and you: Me and you. Look in my eyes. Tonight, touching, contact, don't let go: feel it. Arab? Really? Fuck, I would not have guessed. I've got a lot to learn about this country.

No, I'm not talking about sex.

Fucking is a result of rocking.

Sometimes fucking is a cause of rocking. But it's not the same thing, you feel me, you get me? It's the energy: the energy.

You've got such beautiful hair. But it was your legs in that dress that I couldn't stop looking at. Kick your shoes off. Just kick them off. Let me…

YES! That's right. Hand on my heart, now the other… YES! All right. Stay with me now. Energy. Feel it: here. Now. Run your other hand through your hair.

Fucking Jerusalem. Am I right? Beatles went to Delhi, got it all wrong. Jerusalem should be the home of every rock star. Axel, Springsteen, Mick—they should all be here. With us. Fuck yeah, in my hotel room! Here, in the Holy Land!

Want to know why this is a holy place? Want to know why this is a war zone?

Because this is a high-energy place!

This! Here! Is where the bush burned! This! Here! Is where the walls fell! This! Here! Is where the ark of the covenant was stored and the calves were slaughtered! The home of the Ten Commandments! The place where Jesus came back from the dead!

Unzip me.

Concerts here in the Old City: That's energy! Oh yeah. Oh yeah. Feel my heart, feel my cock. Energy, energy, energy, energy, energy—Yes! Here. Like nothing else in the world, Babe—nothing. So much more money in the States, but here ohhhhhhhhh yes here, just yes, energy—

I learn so much here. Strum me, pluck me, play me, tune me, to the beat of my own heart. Oh I am going to rip your clothes off in…YES!

Squirm! Fight! Kick! If you make me bleed we'll do it again…fuck yeah!

It's always rock and roll, Baby—I told you it's not about the sex. It's about being right next to God and you're the one they're screaming for. I won't stop the music until they shout my name and blow trumpets and I play a power chord and the walls go…. YES! Again! YES!

Oh…you've got it, don't you: couldn't stop even if you…yes. I'm going to put my hand on your heart, see? You can do anything you want, but you've got to keep my hand on your heart, because you've got it now, it was in me, now it's in you, now it's…FUCK! You are gonna get WRECKED!

Ohhhhh…

I am Jewish, actually, by birth. No, I'm not gonna tell you my real name. Even the fucking Internet doesn't know that. I've got secrets. Rock and roll has no secrets, but I've got a few. I can't be a real person and get where I want to go. No, it doesn't stop in Jerusalem. No, no, no, no, no. Oh, no. No, no, no, no, no. Ohhhhh, yes.

All right. I'll tell you something. When you walk out that hotel-room door and it locks behind you…. shhhhh-hhh…let's not kid ourselves. Maybe I'll see you at another show but let's be honest here. I'm going to keep playing until I've got it all—all the verb, all the action. Until I am the shaman who can walk on clouds, call the lightning, burn the bush—Bitch!—until it will hurt you to bite me worse than it hurts me to be bitten…

I've got so much to learn here…

Listen! This is all you get! Hand on my heart! This is what you write on your blog or whatever you're going to do!

I'm going to Everest. I am going to summit Mount Everest, and then take everything I've got, everything you've given me, and go higher. I'm going to be the shaman who can walk on clouds, and fly up even higher where nobody's ever gone. That's the dream.

Why? Seriously? Why?

So that the whole world can see me when I fall. So that the crater will be BIG.

You haven't been listening to a word I said. One more time, and then you're OUT!

Hand on my heart.

Watching Movies Alone

AT 3 IN THE MORNING TWO TAXIS STOPPED ON OPPO-site sides of 18th Street between Folsom and South Van Ness. One revved its engine; one flashed its lights. There were no passengers in sight. They crept up to each other with their engines purring. Each driver rolled down his window.

"Seen any good movies?" the black driver asked the Latino one. It was a hostile question.

"Every day," said the Latino driver. "I got Netflix now."

"Everybody's got Netflix now," the black man said. He ran his hand through his graying hair. "It's not the same."

"It's amazing! The documentaries alone are just...you wouldn't believe how much I've learned."

The black driver, of Cab Number 46, which he'd shared with his brother until his brother had moved to Arizona, where it was cheaper, clenched his fists around the steering wheel. "But who do you watch it with?" he asked.

"What do you mean?" The Latino driver tried to remember how long it had been since they'd seen each other. Did they see Lost in Translation in the theater together? With Max and Neema and Jorge and Vic and Yvonne? "I watch them at home," he said.

The driver of number 46 nodded. "You still live alone?"

"Yes." It was a sore subject.

"In that small place?"

"Yeah."

"So when the movie's on, you're alone in the dark."

"Sometimes it's not dark."

"But you're alone."

"Yeah," the Latino driver of cab 57 admitted. "Sometimes I watch them over dinner.

"It's not like it was."

"Well, no…it's not like it was, but…it's better."

That was it. Those were the fighting words. The doors to 46 unlocked. "How's it better?"

57 wasn't taking this. He leaned out the window. "How many times can you go to the movies, man?"

46 had fought this battle before. He knew he was doomed. "Once, maybe twice a week!"

"Yeah? I can do six movies a week, if I want to. Maybe seven, if I'm not doing anything on a weekend. And I'm not limited to the Cineplex crap or the fucking art houses. I can see anything I want. I can see it twice. The whole movie catalog! How's it not better!"

Number 46 shouted. He'd been shouting this to anyone who'd listen, for years. "BUT YOU'RE ALONE!"

57 honked his horn at his antagonist. "It's just the movies! It doesn't mean you don't have any friends!"

46 slapped his fist against his head. "When do you see Yvonne and Neema anymore? Max? Vic? Jorge?" He hesitated a moment before he said it. "I haven't seen you in a year."

57 clenched his fists around the wheel. "I don't have a big enough apartment to host," he said. He thought he had something else to say after that, but nothing came out. He missed his father. "It's just…I'm busy…"

"You can't get Netflix," 46 said. "You can't. That's always the end. The beginning of the end."

"It's just movies," said 57.

"I hate the city," said 46. "I hate it."

57 turned his blinkers off. "I've got to work."

"What am I supposed to do?" 46 shouted. "You've all got Netflix, and I'm sitting in the theater alone!"

"You can see a lot more movies," 57 said as he drove away.

46 honked his horn at him, over and over again, trying to be noticed in the dark.

Yangtze Riverboat

THE ANNOUNCEMENT TO BOARD THE BOAT GOES OUT first in Mandarin, and then in Cantonese, and then, as an afterthought, in English. We haven't yet had a passenger who spoke only English, but it's my boat and my rules, no matter what the Communist Party says.

The proper setting for a riverboat casino, of course, is the mighty Mississippi—and anyone who knew the Mississippi would know I'm not from there. But here, on the Yangtze, I'm just one more ambitious American with a few connections and a dream. Hardly anyone in America pays to go on a riverboat casino cruise anymore, but here it's snapped up by eager Beijing Yuppies because it seems so American. And the Party encourages it because it makes the Yangtze seem tame.

I have a theory that every form of transportation starts as an experiment, flourishes as an essential means to move cargo, and then ends as a tourist attraction. The Erie Canal, the horse drawn carriage, trains…I'm not wrong. This isn't just transportation, either: every castle in Europe started out as a fortification, became a symbol of authority, and ended as a museum. Churches have a similar trajectory, though some of them are still in the middle section.

I walk along the gangplank in my 1870s New Orleans outfit, prop pistol prominently hanging out of my belt, welcoming the gamblers; reminding them that we have slots and cards on three decks, fine dining with celebrity chefs on the fourth, and a musical review on the fifth. I don't mention the honeymoon suites, those are all booked up. Business is brisk. My Mandarin is still basic, but that's fine—I'm really here to be seen, not heard.

The fate of everything in human culture is to end up a tourist attraction. Cemeteries, writers, thinkers, statesmen: we all end up as a kind of cheap commemorative coin. Look, I was here, put me in your pocket. Success comes to the people who recognize that this is the end of all things, and get ahead of it. Give history what it wants. It's the truth, and it's a damn shame.

But it's not the only truth. The Yangtze isn't tame, no matter how many damns they try to build. And my real money will come when the river finally sinks my boat and the insurance kicks in…insurance I could never have gotten if the government wasn't so keen on making a point.

And this pistol in my belt is only supposed to be a prop. It's real, too. For a man in my position, it's important to keep a grasp on reality however you can.

The Setup

THOM DOES A ONE-MAN SHOW AS SIGMUND FREUD. He gets deeply into the part. He really becomes Sigmund Freud, sometimes getting his memory mixed up with incidents from Freud's letters. He's a gifted actor but not an academic: he had to come to me to help him write the script, but that was years ago.

There was an incident, I don't know how it happened, when the booking agent got mixed up and sent him to perform at a Bar Mitzvah in Brooklyn where the family was expecting a clown.

When Thom showed up in a vintage three-piece suit and white beard but without any balloon animals, heated words were exchanged. He compared Mrs. Goldstein to the Vienna Academy of Sciences building and suggested that little Noah's sense of collective guilt over the death of Moses would lead to crippling sexual inhibitions during high school.

The event planner sent Thom to the bar and called in some favors to get a folk trio over. His drinks were free as long as he didn't bother anybody or tell anyone about the mix-up. Ten minutes later he'd already broken the agreement and called me and told me, "Come down here. Sigmund wants to talk."

This kind of thing is why I stopped making friends with actors. I used to get occasional roles off-Broadway, but since I stopped my life's been drama-free.

It took me almost an hour to get there. Big synagogue, lots of stained glass. I slipped in the back like he'd told me to, and went over to the bar in the community room. He was still in costume. I patted him on the shoulder. He looked up at me and his eyes were swimming in gin.

"Carl," he said. "I'm glad you could come. I have much to get off my mind."

"I think I should give you a ride home," I said.

"This is a moment," he said in a thick German accent. "This is the moment it all goes to shit."

"Where are your keys?"

"When you got out of the business," he said, still German, "you still took yourself seriously as an actor, didn't you?"

The bartender came over and I asked for a vodka cran. "It wasn't about craft. I was working out a lot of issues I didn't know I had," I said. "Abandonment issues, narcissism...I never belonged on stage. It was a compulsion."

"It's the only place I belong," he said. "But I can't take myself seriously after this."

"You're having a bad day. Stand up."

I got him to his feet and we left the bar right before my drink came. He held on to my shoulder as I led him out past the cabinet thing where they keep the Torah.

Thom leaned against me and we hobbled out of the synagogue and over to my car. I put him in the back seat so he could stretch out. As I drove away, Noah ran out of his own party to throw rocks at my car. One hit my window.

Thom moaned.

"You'll sleep it off," I said. "You'll be fine."

"Do you know," he said, obviously in pain, "that by the end of my life I was rethinking the Oedipus complex and my early notions of libido?"

"Of course I do."

"We're not driven," he said, as I pulled on to the highway. "We're not pushed. We make choices. Terrible, terrible, choices."

"You seemed to be thinking that," I agreed, "by the end."

I set the cruise control and got comfortable. If traffic wasn't bad this wouldn't take too long. I'd let him sleep it off at my condo instead of in his roach-infested Tribeca flat, which we called the closet.

He moaned. "Carl?" he asked me . "I'm going to have to stop. I'm going to have to change my life. But the show's so good. It has to live on. When I give it up, will you do the show? Take it over?"

And then, to my surprise, I said, "Yes."

I Don't Know

ANDREA ASKED ME IF THIS WAS ALL THERE IS, AND I told her, "I don't know."

Her friend Jessie has hopped from one entry level job to another for fifteen years—spent four years training as a massage therapist and another two years discovering she didn't like it. She didn't like any of it. She hasn't had a boyfriend in a long time—she's scared of penises, she wonders if she's a lesbian, she lives with her parents a lot of the time. Jessie doesn't want to die alone, and she doesn't have anyone important in her life…and we don't know what to do about it.

Andrea's friend Wendy, whom I flirted with in college, has spent twenty years working on a marriage that breaks down every two miles. Andrea won't name the diseases Wendy has contracted from this man. She was finally thinking of divorce when her daughter goes off to school, but her daughter just decided to turn down a SUNY Buffalo scholarship and go to a local community college instead so she'll be closer to her boyfriend. Wendy can't stop crying about it, and calls all her friends on the phone, and no one knows what to say.

Andrea's friend David graduated late from college, then worked for five years at a job he hated and left to go to grad school: it was his ticket out. It took him another four years to get his masters in graphic design, and now he's out of work. Even the temp agency where he made his rent while he got through school can't find work for him. He's thinking about the army, but he's a geeky blue-state kid and we're afraid the army will kill him. "Maybe I'll go to law school," he says, and we look at each other and try not to sigh.

Andrea has a steady job that, three out of five days, she likes. She's saved up a lot of money, and if the state doesn't go bankrupt she'll have a pension in 30 years. She's learning to carve and stain glass because we all need an outlet. Sometimes she comes over. Sometimes we kiss. Sometimes she's stays the night. She tells me about Jessie and Wendy and David, and she's noticed her first gray hair. One night when she refused to eat dinner and she refused to take her clothes off and she refused to leave me alone, she demanded to know: "Is this all there is? Does it ever get better?"

I told her, "I don't know."

"Maybe," I said, "you should take a trip. Maybe you should go to Spain. Maybe you should visit the Alhambra, and after you've seen the exquisite tiles and the minarets and heard the story about how Muslims, Christians, and Jews were able to live in peace together that one time in history, you can go to a nearby coffee shop and you can order tea and have it sweetened with mint leaves and you can watch the sun set over the temple and hear '80s music coming from a nearby club…and then you can decide, as the Moroccan waiter looks at the way your hair tumbles over your shoulders, if you want to go dancing."

She takes a deep breath, and she cries a little. We sit down together and she puts her head on my shoulder, and asks me to tell her another story.

The Time Travelers of San Francisco

THE CAMERA CAUGHT YOU UNAWARE, JUST AFTER you'd applied your makeup, dressed like a 1920s gypsy performer. A steam punk vagabond with an artsy streak, eyeing the mini-bar and smoking in the hotel suite I rented for us all to meet and get into costume before heading off to the annual Time Travelers Ball.

We were a motley assortment; Chris was channeling J. Edgar Hoover, down to the pistol under his jacket and women's underwear in his pants. Alba was a 17th century witch about to be burned at the stake, her face pale... such a perfectionist she even scented her hair to smell like smoke. Deborah was a colonial wife from a Jamaican plantation; she was working through some issues by taking on the identity of the people who had oppressed her family. (I wonder, now, how that worked out.) Alex was a monk and Emily was Joan of Arc (that's two women who were going to burn). Alan was a knight in shining armor: completely inaccurate historically, he would be mocked mercilessly all night.

This was the last moment before it went wrong for us. I took that picture of you before we all piled into the limo and were driven across San Francisco to the Old Mint. We didn't have to wait in line because I knew a guy who knew a guy…we skipped right past the World War II soldiers and the 1960s go-go dancers and the 1950s housewives and the Roman legions and were let inside by a pair of Dutch botanists manning the velvet rope.

We separated at the absinthe bar and never got to dance. I followed a Venetian courtesan up to the balcony and traded stories about the Sacred City of Prester John, leaning in closer and closer until I brushed her hair away so that my lips could reach her ear. Her hands drifted onto my thigh.

I saw you down below, on the ballroom floor, waltzing with a tall young man in a tuxedo sporting a goofy grin. Even from this distance I could see that he wasn't one of us; it was obvious in the poor fit of his costume and the sincerity of his smile. I watched you spinning and went on with the seduction at hand…I cannot resist a woman who carries poison in her glove.

If I had known that you would never come up to the balcony because you were afraid of heights…if I had known you would briefly fall in love with this boy…if I had known how difficult you would find it to let go of someone who loved you unreservedly, if badly…if I had known that the scorn I felt for him would come between us like a trench in war because you, too, felt judged…

If I had known these things, I would have put aside the delights of Venice during the Crusades. I would have run past the inventors of the locomotive and down the stairs filled with orphan chimney sweeps. I would have spun into the waltz and walked you off the dance floor in a straight line, taken you outside, and given you a cigarette.

I would have laughed with you at the folly of our hearts, and the way they lead us down false paths and garden steps lined with roses that will not live through the night. I would have let you land gently from the heights of this world I should never have invited you into, and left a trail of pebbles between us on solid ground, so that I could find you again as you wandered through the offices and taxis where you really feel at home, restlessly traveling from home to home, job to job, man to man, but never looking up.

I would have done this for you, instead of climbing to the next balcony with my courtesan, and then the roof, rising ever closer to the constellations. And now for all the space between us there is no room for a second chance.

Dark Enchantment

I CAME ALL THAT WAY JUST TO MEET A WICKED LIT-
tle man. A flight to London, where an antique bookseller
from a family of Nazi sympathizers gave me an address in
Gottingen. A train to Paris, and then to Germany, where
the collector of dueling swords and pistols suggested I go
no further because he had never seen anyone come back.
But he gave me the name of a village in exchange for a
hundred Euros.

Another train, this time to Prague, where a chorus of
prostitutes sang drinking songs outside of my hotel window at 3 a.m., and then another across the long expanse
to St. Petersburg. I bumped into an old friend there, a
man I hadn't seen in 15 years, who bought me dinner at
his hotel and blushingly admitted, after too much wine,
that he had come here to find a wife.

"I failed. I can't find love in America," he said, tears in
his eyes. "I don't know what I'm doing wrong. I don't...get
it." He knew the young, beautiful, girls of Russia were a
bad fit for him—but nobody's really happy with a consola-
tion prize.

From there a plane to Novosibirsk, and then a train to
Biysk, where the natives stared at me through their pale
eyes. From there I had to rent a car to drive east—thank

God it was summer. I told everyone I was going to Kyzyl, so that the bandits they were sure to have ambush me would be thrown off my trail.

The cave was a dozen miles outside Orovesk, just like the collector had told me. I walked down a steep trail that crossed an underground river and then up into a valley covered in fog. I walked down a gravel path and everywhere heard the calling of birds, but saw no wings; I heard the neighing of horses, but not hoof beats.

The cottage was a mile further down than I'd been told, but they say time and space are relative to the observer. Perhaps I, personally, was just farther away than anyone had thought.

The little man was roasting an animal on a sword over a fire pit in the back. Burnt pots and pans were scattered on the ground. For some reason he only spoke French to me, although I'm sure he didn't need to.

"You've come this far," he told me, "but I think you want to go farther." His eyes took in the road that curled past his cottage.

I shook my head. I told him what I wanted. I told him it was for my wife. He chuckled, and said that the advantage of living so close to the edge of the world is that he knows at a glance how desperate his customers must be. He knew I would do anything. I thought he was right.

I had not understood what that meant. You learn so much about yourself when someone has you at their mercy.

I learned that, for me, love was not enough. I fled before my debt was really paid, leaving two fingers and an ear with him. Leaving more, honestly, but these are the wounds

114

you can see—and so I can't avoid talking about them. The invisible scars are the ones I keep to myself.

I traveled back, covered in bandages, and spent a week in Orovesk recovering. We had no language in common, but they knew what had happened: they teach the young girls and the old men how to tend to wounds like mine. Their eyes were sympathetic, but I always turned away.

No one in Biysk recognized me when I returned the car. I went to Moscow, and from there directly to New York.

I stayed in a bar until 2 in the morning, and then went home. I kissed my wife on the cheek while she lay in bed, and as she woke up, emerging from her dreams, I said I was sorry that I couldn't do it. That there were, in fact, some things I would sacrifice her to protect—and that I hadn't known.

She smiled, and hugged me, and said she was so sorry I had been hurt, she'd never wanted that, and we lay weeping together. We fell asleep, and I slept for more than 20 hours, dreaming of rivers and rainbows and white gowns. She took a fatal dose of heroin while I lay there and was cold in my arms when I woke up.

Body and Blood

LILIES ARE THE FLOWERS OF DEATH THAT YOU GIVE to a corpse to match the pallor of decay. Roses are the flowers of love that you give to a sweetheart to match the veneer of passion. Violets are the flowers of sadness, and tulips are the flowers that bloom for seductions without love. For every mood there is a flower. Even nightshade.

No common weed, this, but a flower of potency. I have always suspected that if you grind enough roses into a concentrate, you will get a love potion. But nightshade doesn't require that much work. It is what it is, the flower of murder, and it is the most honest flower of all.

I cut the stems gently with my steel scissors while wearing white gloves. We should all be so honest. We should all be so direct. Instead we spend our days avoiding conflict and our nights crying into our pillows. We should follow the nightshade. Let any who touch us wrongly die.

I arrange the plants in their indigo vase, shape them into a bouquet. Sprinkle little wildflowers—pretty things—as adornments where the color needs contrast. Fill the water to just the right level: after it has steeped enough it will also be toxic to drink, if anyone is stupid enough to try.

The smell of the bouquet alone is enough to induce lightheadedness, even seizures in the very weak. Beauty

117

of this kind is not for the weak. I do not give my gifts to the weak. That never works out.

The bell rings. I step back and survey the bouquet quickly. I nod. Yes. Yes. This murderous instrument is an affirmation of life, a statement that splendor is possible under any circumstances. I am moved and choke up for a moment. Yes. Yes. I walk over to the wall and press the button to buzz my guest in.

Of course I know who it is. No one ever drops by unexpectedly. No one ever checks in just to see how I'm doing, if I want to grab a bite or talk. The people who love me most are the most afraid of me. They keep a respectful distance. It's why I hate them most of all.

Solitude gives me an air of mystery that I have never deserved. People never understand that monsters can have aesthetic sentiments too. I wonder when that happened. I have occasionally leafed through old records from the Renaissance, wondering if there was a moment when Leonardo or Raphael said something about evil understanding beauty. I go to the kitchen and boil water for tea. I have quite the collection of teas from around the world, but my favorites come from a small patch of land that was once a slave plantation just across the river in the Ninth Ward. Like nightshade, it is potent: a single cup lingering on my tongue for hours, ruining the flavor of anything sweet.

There is a knock on my apartment door. "It's open!" I say. Of course it is: Who would come by unexpectedly?

She opens the door and steps in, her hard boots making almost no noise against my creaky wooden floor.

"Sister," I say.

She smiles, a little bit, at the title. She's been defrocked for a long time, but likes it when someone remembers.

She notes two new paintings in the hallway: perhaps she suspects that the scenes of the suffering of martyrs are mixed in real blood.

"You've been hard at work," she says.

"Yes." I'm annoyed by the remark. What else would I be doing?

"What do you have for me?"

I point to the table, though it should be obvious: the lights are set up around it. It's the centerpiece of my living room. The eye is immediately drawn to it. Is she being polite or sarcastic?

She steps over, her long white fur coat rustling. She looks it over. She smells it and swoons with pain. She runs her black leather gloved hands over it gently.

She looks me closely in the eyes—mine brown, hers green—and speaks without lies or flattery: "It is beautiful."

"Thank you."

We are silent for a moment and then my foot begins to tap.

She nods. "It is a peculiar gift you have," she says.

"I know," I snap.

She raises her eyebrows. "I have never met anyone else with your talents."

"I'm sure."

"Given enough time," she says, "I think you would redeem all of hell by making art out of fire and skin."

"Given enough time," I agree. "Sister, do you have it!"

She smiles. My impatience pleases her. I must remember that she, too, is a poison thing. No one else could make the journey she has.

"Of course."

My voice catches. "Give it to me."

She raises her eyebrows again and I kneel. I hold out my hands. I look up at her face.

From inside her coat she produces a small gold box. She snaps it open and removes a thin cracker, a sacred thing. I stick out my tongue and she places it there, where it melts into my spit and muscle. She takes out a small glass vial, holding red wine. She puts it in my hands and I drink it all.

She places her hand on my head. "You are forgiven," she says. "There is a place in heaven for even such as you."

I collapse on the floor, gasping and sobbing with relief and she steps over me to pick up the bouquet. She lets herself out, as I weep and cry and rend my clothes.

I will not be abandoned.

To Look Inside

SHE LIES SLEEPING ON WHITE SHEETS UNDER RED blankets. Her raven hair is spread across the pillows, but of the man there is no trace.

This is a tricky moment: she'll be angry if I don't clean the room promptly every morning, but she'll be angry if I wake her. Her anger is dangerous. Even when she sleeps, there is something of the snake in her. I take a deep breath and remind myself that fear is normal. If I didn't want this, I shouldn't have volunteered.

I can't help comparing her hair to mine, again. They're both dark. They're both long. But that's the only resemblance. She's pale. She's svelte. She's curved in just a way that draws the eye along the body. She's toned and shapely. I have so much to learn.

He was good looking, this one, but he must have been smart, too: she never brings them here if they're not smart. I caught a glimpse of him last night as they opened the first bottle of wine: he smiled at me and something in it was sad. Resigned. I almost think he knew what was going to happen and decided to do it anyway.

I take another deep breath, pull out my dust cloth and tiptoe into the room. The sunlight has preceded me. I must be quiet and fast.

I do the shelves first, the furthest thing in the room from her. I dust in time to her breaths. I spray the cloth first and then wipe the surface, careful not to touch the glass figurines from Venice or the puppets from Japan, then run the cloth along. Good. Easy. I look back, and she hasn't moved.

When the man saw me last night and smiled, he wasn't flirting. At all.

I don't know how I'll ever learn to do what she does. Someday, she says, she'll teach me. That's where this is going. But sometimes I think she's lying. She always lies.

Outside the room, a cat jumps down a staircase and lands with a thud. Move! Don't linger. I go to the nightstand next, the closest thing to her head. I shiver as I lift up the alarm clock…it hasn't been wound in over a year at least…and I dust underneath. The crystal decanter with I don't know what inside: it looks like water, but nothing is so simple here. It's heavier than it looks.

I pull back after that. It's not finished, but my hands are shaking. I'm too scared to do it right. Better that I get it half done, and hope she's satisfied…since she's still asleep. Yes, that's my best chance. I tiptoe over to the dresser. The cat jumps again and I nearly scream.

The dresser's easy. One long big surface, such beautiful wood. Someday, I will have furniture like this. Someday, men like that one…men of all kinds, men who have never looked at me twice…will come to my house, and try too hard to flirt with me, and will fall under my spell even before they've drunk my wine. Someday. It will be worth it. All this will be worth it, then.

Besides, what else am I going to do? It's too easy to grow old and alone. My mother taught me, without ever once saying so, that life is cruel to the kind.

Done. That's everything, except...except...

Oh God, I can't do that. I can't.

And yet, I'm tiptoeing over to the cabinet. The special one, with the silver hinges and the golden lock. The one I have been instructed never to touch.

But I have.

She's sleeping, I can't do this: if I open it right in front of her while she's sleeping, she'll kill me if she wakes up. She'll kill me, or worse. None of my dreams will come true. But I can't help myself. The lock is easy to open from the outside. I can't turn away, I can't stop. I'm too afraid, and I want it too much, and if I were wise enough to leave well enough alone I wouldn't be here.

Gently, in time with her breathing, I open up the cabinet door, and I see them. In their little glass bubbles, frozen, alive, in clear paperweights—I see the men.

The one from last night is there, looking around, crying and hugging his knees. She's already put a label beside him—Antonio, poet. A poet! She's wanted a poet for a long time, but they've never been good enough. I suppose he's good enough. He sees me, and pounds on the glass, but it doesn't make a sound, and of course I'm not going to help him. I wouldn't know how.

Roger the CEO also pounds the floor of his glass prison, and Donald the machinist stares, they all stare, wondering what is going to happen next. Wondering how they followed the beautiful woman's curves across New

Orleans and into a prison of glass, one night's passion all it took to turn them into collectibles. Their eyes all follow me, my every move, their mouths imploring.

I take a deep breath. Take it all in. I can do this. I can do this.

I close the cabinet door and lock it softly. I turn around, my breath catching, to see if my mistress has moved. Thank God she is still asleep.

I look at her curves again, her glorious curves, and her magic hands.

She and I have the same hair. Someday, this will be me.

Vaclav's Inheritance

THE LIBRARY WAS DARK. THE LIBRARY WAS CLOSED. Its walls were books.

The caretaker arrived at dawn and looked for a way in. He started by examining the front door, which was entirely barricaded by Proust. Then he looked for cracks in the windows, which were mostly comedies of manners about people looking through windows. He ran his hands over the leather covers slowly, slipping his fingers as far as he could into the bindings, just the way his father had taught him, and been taught by his grandfather. They'd been trying to get in for a very long time.

After acknowledging again that all the windows were impenetrable, he went to the vents. The vents were made of the classics of post-structural criticism, and were different every time he looked at them. A few of the translations were poor enough to be loose, and he wiggled, then pulled, then threw himself against them again and again. Someday, he was sure, they would break open, and there might be a crawl space to wiggle through.

"Tomorrow," he told himself, "I'm going to burn the thing down." He said that fairly often. He assumed the library was flammable, it was made of paper, though in his secret dreams there wasn't even an ember when he doused it in vodka and threw firecrackers on the roof.

He shook his head and went to see how his son was progressing on the tunnel. In a few more years, they might have a way to the foundation.

His great-grandfather had bought the property from a Slovakian baron 20 years before the Great War. He didn't know much else, because his father and grandfather had told different stories about how it happened. In one version, great-grandfather was a hero, cleverly outwitting the nobleman; in another, he was a fool. He paused on the way to the tunnel, to once again admire the slant of the ceiling, which was covered in Tarot cards. Even from this distance, he could make them out perfectly despite 100 years of winters: the Emperor, the Hanged Man, the Devil.

They had been lucky in the Great War: two of his great uncles had been conscripted and sent to the trenches where one had died of mustard gas and one had been cut in two by a machine gun, but they hadn't lost the land. The fighting had happened 80 miles north and 90 miles west, but not here. The roads had been littered with land mines, but not here. Everything had been quiet around the library.

Not the second time. In the second war they'd had to cover the library with swastikas because the damn Nazis had marched right by. The SS had driven their cars just over that hill and the soldiers marching behind them had shouted out deadly slogans, and everyone knew the Nazis burned books. For a moment the world had stood still as the eyes of the unstoppable Reich looked over them—but they had not seen past the flags.

It had been his job to keep it safe from the Communists, who claimed that the library belonged to everyone, then talked about knocking it over and using the land for a factory to make shoes. He'd been interrogated three times and put in prison for a year. But when he came back, they hadn't found a way in either. He smiled, his face crinkling like a vulture's. He'd loved the library, then. He'd loved the fact that there was something even the state couldn't crack. Back then, it had given him hope.

Now, he wanted to crack it too. He was sick of the mystery.

It puzzled him, terrified him, to think that many of the books of the library had been written while it was in his family's care. The post-structuralist works, for example: they had all been published while he was coming up with excuses to tell the secret police, explaining why there wasn't a simple key that would open the door, or why a rock wouldn't fly through the windows. These books, the ones here, had come first. There were, he was sure, books not yet published in plain sight, if he knew what to look for. He shuddered, trying to understand this grotesque act of plagiarism.

He saw that his son had stopped digging. It was not warm, but his shirt was off, his dark skin stained with sweat, his eyes closed.

"Vaclav," he said, "it's not yet noon."

His son threw his spade down into the dirt. "Father," he said, "I'm done."

"Are you sick?"

His son didn't answer. They both knew what he had really meant.

"If we keep digging, we can get under it. Maybe the floor isn't so strong."

Vaclav looked away.

"I'll get you some water," he told his son. He walked towards the well. The young today...they had no sense of history. Or of the sacrifices others had made for them. They had no priorities. They were easily dazzled by the things they saw on television, hypnotized by the idea of a better life.

He turned the crank and sent the bucket careening down into the old stone well. His son was being lied to by the West, by America, which didn't have any buildings over 300 years old, which thought that power made them free. If they'd lived under Communism, they would know that power doesn't make you free.

The bucket hit the water and sank. He pulled on the crank, so much heavier now, and began to reel the bucket up.

"Father!" Vaclav called.

"Almost ready," he called back. He dipped the cup in the bucket and drank the water deeply himself. Then he filled the cup again and turned around.

It was time to have the talk. Perhaps.

Every generation had to get the talk, eventually.

He hoped he could remember the words.

He walked back to the tunnel, holding the cup. It was hotter out than he'd thought.

"Pavel and Dmitri are going to start a software company in Prague," Vaclav said, taking the water. "We can make good money with all the European companies outsourcing."

"And the American ones," he mumbled.

"That's right," said Vaclav, sipping the water, then drinking deeply. "Good money."

"And Masha is in Prague," he told his son, his voice hardening.

Vaclav looked away. "That's not important."

"You never really get over your first love."

"I will."

The father nodded. "You think you can do anything when you're young. You think that human nature is being discovered for the first time and history is just being written." These were the words. These were the words his father had told him. Just over the hill, over his shoulder, the iron curtain was ready to descend.

"There's a better life," said Vaclav. "This…" he gestured at the library. His voice trembled. His hand shook. He'd been digging this tunnel for six years. Almost a third of his life had been spent with a shovel in his hand. "This is just…" he looked away. "I can't do this anymore."

"But you're wrong," said the father. "Because the story is old, and already written, and nothing ever changes. Do you understand? Whatever you do, the script is already written. If you go to Prague, you will not have any land. You will not have any family. You will be no one, starting over. And you will open every door and climb through every window looking for something that will give you a place again." This was the talk. "But the inside of every building will be empty. You will walk through every archway in Prague, and find nothing inside. Because it has all been opened, and prodded, and explored, and mankind is still mad with grief."

His son's eyes were wide.

He gestured back to the library. "But not this. This is the only mystery left, Vaclav, and it has endured. Maybe I will not live to see it opened. Maybe you will not live to see it opened. But this is the only script we do not know the ending to."

Vaclav tried to look away, but his father was firm.

"And the freedom you feel making choices that do not matter, unmooring yourself from an enduring mystery, will…"

He stopped. The father stopped.

His mouth flapped up and down. His wiped his brow.

In panic, he realized, he'd forgotten the words. He didn't know how the talk ended. He couldn't remember.

"Will…" he tried to improvise. "Son…" he could tell his son was ready to weep, but now…"Vaclav"…now he could catch a glimmer of hope streaking back into his eyes. "Don't leave me, son. Your arms are strong, the tunnel…the tunnel could work…"

He couldn't remember how the talk ended. It always ended the same way. He had no idea.

"Father," Vaclav said, "the library will be here if I come back. If I miss it. You'll be here. You'll always be here, I know."

"That's…that's not how it works…" His father tried to clear his head.

But Vaclav put his hand on his shoulder. "I'm sorry, but my train leaves tomorrow morning. I will call. I promise."

Vaclav stepped away from the tunnel. Saw that his father was going to speak. "Please don't make this hard… harder," he said.

He watched Vaclav walk away then, back to the house where his mother waited, his mother who undoubtedly knew. He looked back at the library, and then at his distant son. This wasn't how it ended. He knew that. This wasn't how it went. There are some things that can't be changed. He just couldn't remember how it had to go. And now his son would have to learn it all over again.

He looked back at the library, at the walls of Dante and Petrarch, the siding of James Joyce, the pavings of Umberto Eco.

His son would have to learn it all over again. Generations would be lost. He shook his head and picked up the shovel. His shoulders already hurt. Maybe he could make it inside in time.

Women and Spiders

THE SAN FRANCISCO MUNI TRAIN LURCHES AROUND a corner and Irene takes her hand out of my lap to point. "Look, a spider!"

It's a difficult balance with Irene. It's only when we're both drunk...but just drunk enough...that we fall into each other's arms.

"A spider," she says again, her speech slurred by bourbon. "Inside the train!"

I shrug. I want her hand back in my lap. "It probably wants to go to the Outer Sunset."

She turns her head. "Is this the right train for that?"

"Uh huh."

"Wait," she says, "that doesn't make sense."

She gets up. "I'm going to help it," she says.

With surprising care for someone who can't walk straight, she scoops the spider onto her hand as the train doors open and two people at the other end get out. The spider crawls around to the back of her hand as she rushes out the open door, gently pushes it onto the sidewalk, and then staggers back in.

The door closes behind her and she collapses back into her seat. She puts her head on my shoulder.

"Did you see that?" she asks. "I saved it."

The train lurches forward and our heads collide. We both say "Sorry."

"You what?" I ask.

"I'm sorry," she says.

"No, you what? Before that?"

"I saved that spider," she says. "Did you see?"

"How did you...?" I close my eyes. "How did you do that?"

"I put it outside," she says. "Where it will be safe."

"Are you kidding?" I ask.

She gives me an angry shove. "It's a living creature," she says as the train rolls to the next stop sign. "It deserves to be saved."

I open my eyes and put my hand on her shoulder. "Just because it's an animal doesn't mean it's safer outside."

"It wasn't safe in here." The train starts up again.

"You put it in a completely new environment. It doesn't know where to nest. It doesn't know what the predators are, or where they are. It has to start all over."

She's looking at me the wrong way. I need to stop this. Why can't I stop this?

"You were a catastrophe for it," I say. "Like an earthquake, or a tornado."

She pulls away from my hand. She leans forward to yell at me more effectively. "I...saved...it."

I lean in too, but not to yell. I like it when we're close. I should change the subject, but I'm on a track. My mouth is being pulled along by my mind.

"That poor spider must be so confused. First it ended up on a train, a wholly alien environment, moving around in a

134

way it can't understand. Then, just when it's trying to make itself safe, you grab it and put it in another new place, like nowhere it's ever seen, one more thing its instincts weren't made to process, and it has to start from scratch."

"But it's SAFER there," she says, almost spitting when she shouts. "It's meant to be outdoors."

"You wouldn't be safer in the Amazon rain forest," I say. "If spiders pass stories on to their descendants, this would be the great upheaval, the Fall from Eden. Old Testament stuff. Angels with flaming swords."

She opens her mouth.

"Ah," she says. "Ah."

But words don't come. The train barrels around a curve and we both tumble in opposite directions. When I focus again, she's curled into herself, closed off from me. It's the only way she has to punish me, whether she knows it or not.

I lean forward.

She turns away.

"Oh, come on." I reach out. "We're having fun." Her back stiffens. My hand stops. We're spiraling now. I can see it. But I can't stop talking.

"You didn't SAVE the spider! You saw a situation, and did what you wanted to do, and didn't think it through, just like you always do!"

She gets up and moves two rows of seats down. We're not recovering from this tonight.

"Look…" I say, and get up to follow.

The train comes to a stop. I stumble. Irene jumps up and walks to the door. Kicks the mechanism, and when the door swooshes open she jumps out onto the sidewalk, into the darkness of a residential neighborhood in the middle of nowhere.

She turns around. "Fuck you!" she says. "I'm erasing your number from my phone!"

"Oh, come on…" I say from inside the train. And then I decide I don't want to be pathetic. "There won't be any more trains!" I say. "You'll never get a cab out here! Get back on the train!"

"Fuck you!" she says.

And now I don't want to be reasonable, either, and this will hurt more than the hangover in the morning. "You never listen to anybody! You just go with your instincts! You're just a spider too!"

She gives me the finger with both hands and after the door closes between us she turns her back on the train as it takes me away, towards civilization. I look back at her as best I can. I don't think we're going to get past this.

Journey

MY GRANDFATHER WAS THE PASTOR OF A SMALL congregation in Brooklyn. Everybody he knew and loved could be found in a ten-block radius. When someone moved to Manhattan, it broke his heart. When someone moved to Long Island, they were dead to him. I asked him once, "Grandpa, how can you love a God who is present in the stars of distant galaxies billions and billions of light years away?" He told me that Grandma's kitchen is really the center of the universe, and that all miracles begin by simmering on her stove.

My dad broke his father's heart, becoming a hippie and joining a back-to-the-land commune on the Missouri side of the Ozark mountains. It was 1970; he was chasing a girl. That girl and her strawberry blond hair and freckles had decided that you couldn't really live unless you got back to nature. It amazes me that Dad would leave his father's ten blocks—ten blocks where all doors opened to him, ten blocks where he was a prince with a divine lineage—because he wanted to be with that girl. I've never loved anyone that way. He wasn't even sure he'd get her. There were almost 100 people on that 40-acre commune, and the love was as free as the birds. "I believed in your mom," he told me. "I believed in us."

The farmers around them didn't like the hippies, and most of them didn't stay. By the time I was born Mom and Dad were the only back-to-the-landers left on the land, and I grew up in a 40-acre paradise, my sisters and me throwing our clothes off when we went out in the morning and finding them again after dark, before dinner. Dad built a sauna, a hot tub, and a little observatory to bring us even closer to the stars of distant galaxies. We could already see them with our naked eyes. Mom sits on the deck of the house Dad built for her, surrounded by nature. Dad never sits more than 10 feet away from her. They're happy.

I know I broke their hearts when I moved away, but where Grandpa had roared at the end of the world they whimpered. They'd already set this in motion themselves. They knew it was coming: like father like son. I went to school in Los Angeles and eventually moved to Brooklyn. I got lucky: I have a rent-controlled loft space. I'm trying to get attention for my multi-media quilting: I hang long quilts from the rafters and then project video on them from nooks in the wall. The video images interact with the elements on the quilt so, for instance, if I make a quilt of a journey across the mountains, the video image will be different people crossing those quilted mountains, the space worked out exactly so that they nearly fall off the ravines and have to cover their heads under the storm clouds and shiver when they reach the snow-capped top. My most successful quilts are scenes from religious texts: my image of Rama fighting demons to free Sita, and Gilgamesh journeying to the underworld, and Moses leading the children of Israel across the Red Sea. It's hard for an artist to get attention. Some days I feel like I'd slit my best friend's throat to get my name in the Huffington Post. Some days, I'm sure my best friends would slit mine. When I talk to my parents, they don't understand when I tell them that I don't really trust anyone I know. They just don't...process...that.

I don't know what else I'd do, though: I mean, if I wasn't an artist then...what?

My grandpa's church is gone, an early victim of gentrification, before people knew how to stop it: the old neighborhood replaced by condos. At night, I can open one of my windows and crawl out on top of another building's roof and stare at the space where his church used to be, 14 blocks away. I look up at the sky, but here there are no stars.

I have so much passion, and no idea what I'm doing with my life.

Afterword

THANKS AND APPRECIATION MUST GO, FIRST AND last, to Cary Tennis, who has created and led the only writing workshops that I have ever enjoyed, let alone gotten something out of. Cary creates spaces and communities in which artists have the freedom to experiment and grow, and his unique combination of honest humility and extraordinary talent make him a better catalyst for creativity than any school or studio. This book happened because Cary Tennis believed in me.

Janet Shepard's indispensable editing makes my writing better. That is a skill. The fact that she makes the editing process so painless, even effortless, is a gift. I am actively looking for another project we can work on together.

Of the many writers who've influenced me the one I am most excited about thanking is Florence King, who I fear stands largely unrecognized as one of the great essayists of the latter half of the 20th century. Her writing is so polished as to seem completely natural only to anyone who has not tried to be so eloquent in so few words. Her example moved me away from the rococo embellishments of my college years and towards a deep love of classical simplicity in art. She's done all my readers a tremendous service.

Thanks are also owed to Jeff Barron, who is indirectly responsible for the opportunity that launched me on my short career of international night-life reporting, the experience of which significantly influenced this book. Jeff has the added distinction of being my oldest friend in the world.

I'm also grateful to my parents, Mary Campbell and Ted Wachs, for putting up with me during my difficult childhood, difficult adolescence, painful college years, thorny graduate school experience, the extremely trying years when I would call every few months to mention I was now in Istanbul, or Moscow, or Jerusalem, the complicated years of my early reporting career, the tough time of my cross-country move, and now...when everything's fine and I never call. You've been my champions.

The rest of you will just have to wait until my next book. Except for Karen. She gets thanked now. Thank you, Karen.

About the Author

DURING COLLEGE BENJAMIN WACHS LIVED IN A Buddhist monastery in India. After dropping out of graduate school, he worked as a freelance nightlife reporter for *Playboy.com*. Traveling around the world, he wrote about bars for money and spontaneously sang sacred music in some of history's greatest cathedrals for fun. The police were called to stop his singing in the cathedral of King's College Cambridge (but didn't catch him), while the guards at the Vatican shrugged and let him continue. After he sang in the temple of Hagia Sophia in Istanbul, a museum guide told him he represents everything wrong with American culture, but he was hired to entertain pilgrims in Jerusalem.

Currently he is the bar columnist for *San Francisco Weekly*. His work has been published in *Village Voice Media*, on *National Public Radio,* and numerous local newspapers and small magazines. To read more of his work and learn about his upcoming publications and performances, visit *www.TheWachsGallery.com*.

This is his first collection of fiction.

www.ingramcontent.com/pod-product-compliance
Lightning Source LLC
Chambersburg PA
CBHW060423260626
47161CB00005B/1756